The ARIZONA Kid

The ARIZONA *Kid*

RON KOERTGE

FIC.
K78a

Joy Street Books
LITTLE, BROWN and COMPANY
BOSTON   TORONTO

Library of Congress Cataloging-in-Publication Data

Koertge, Ronald.
The Arizona kid.

Summary: Sixteen-year-old Billy comes to terms with his own values when he
is sent to live with his gay uncle in Tucson and is introduced to the world of
rodeos where he falls in love with an outspoken racehorse rider named Cara.
[1. Rodeos — Fiction.   2. Homosexuality — Fiction.
3. Arizona — Fiction]   I. Title.
PZ7.K8187Ar 1988   [Fic]   87-35361
ISBN 0-316-50101-8

10 9 8 7 6 5 4 3 2 1

VB

Published simultaneously in Canada
by Little, Brown & Company (Canada) Limited

Printed in the United States of America

The ARIZONA Kid

1

When the train stopped in Tucson, everybody else got their stuff together and jammed the aisles, but I ducked into the bathroom and put Sunblock 15 on every inch of exposed skin I owned. I knew I'd miss saying goodbye to a couple of girls I'd made friends with on the trip, but they were a little older than me, anyway. And a lot taller.

My mom had put the whammy on me about the sun, so I was pretty greasy by the time I made my way through the empty coach, stood on the arm rest, and found my bag on the overhead rack. In the paper sack next to it was the straw hat I'd promised to wear, the one with the fish on the band.

I put it on and got the suitcase. When I dropped the suitcase because my hands were so slick from Sunblock, my hat — which now seemed a lot bigger than it did back in Missouri — tilted forward and blinded me as I struggled down the stairs. I felt the porter grab my elbow. "Thanks," I muttered into the brim.

Was it hot! I could feel the concrete through the bottoms of my new Air Jordans (on sale for $19.95, down from $50). My hands were full, but I managed to tilt the hat back and take a look around: red tile, brown adobe, an Indian with a bandanna around his head sitting by a guy in a leather vest and scuffed-up boots. Cowboys and Indians.

I was in the West. The Old West. The Wild West! I couldn't help myself: as much as I wanted to be cool and nonchalant, my stomach was fluttery. A whole summer in a new place; a place away from my parents (who I loved, but, let's face it, parents are parents); a place so hot the girls probably wore bikinis to church; a place where I'd take a giant step toward my childhood dream: becoming a vet. A place where — who knows? — anything might happen.

I set the bags down. Where was Uncle Wes? I didn't bother to dig out the picture; I had it memorized. Slick black hair, great tan, perfect teeth. I looked around woozily: nobody who fit that description. Nobody, in fact, anywhere.

Down at the end of the platform a van pulled up and someone hurried toward me. Whoever it was looked like one of those mirages you see in the summer, just a shape in the shimmery heat.

"Billy?"

It was somebody calling to me from a mile away.

"I'm your Uncle Wes." He offered his hand, I remember that much. And that I put mine out even though it weighed a ton.

He grabbed, but my fingers were still so slick from the sunblock that they shot out of his grip and I went down in a heap.

*   *   *

Everything was cool when I came to. And white, like the inside of an igloo. My bare arm was lying on cool white tile, there was something cool on my forehead. I looked up into cool blue eyes, and a cool hand picked up mine.

"You fainted," said Wes. "No big deal."

Fainted? Oh, yeah. From the heat. The heat in Tucson. Where I was staying the summer with my uncle. My *gay* uncle. In whose lap I had my head.

"Holy shit!" I yelled as I shot to my feet and stood gasping between the sinks in the train station's men's room.

"I think," Wes reassured a porter and a couple of other people who'd been watching, "it's safe to say he's regained consciousness."

"I'll have the air conditioning on in just a second," Wes said as he pulled out of the Amtrak parking lot. "You take some deep breaths."

"I'm sorry about how I acted back there."

"Forget it."

I squinted as we coasted down what was probably Burning Drive and hung left at Scalding Way. Wes wore three silver bracelets on his right wrist. As he drove they clinked together,

"You sell those, don't you?" I asked, glad to change the subject.

"Uh-huh, and baskets and rugs and beadwork and artifacts." He grinned at me. "Take one," he said, slipping a bracelet off.

"No, really."

"Just see if you like it."

I'd never worn a bracelet before. A watch, but not a bracelet. In Bradleyville, Missouri, guys in bracelets are few and far between. Like nonexistent. Still, it looked okay. It was a heavy one, wide, with a wavy design on it. A guy's bracelet. I was really pale, so it didn't look as good as it did on Wes. And it wobbled on my wrist, though it'd been snug on his.

"I know what you need," he said. "A Coke. When I was sixteen a Coke would fix almost anything."

"I could use a Coke."

"Did you get any sleep on the train?"

"Some."

But not when Laura dozed off with her head on my shoulder. First of all, I didn't want to wake her up by my nodding out, too, and banging heads like a couple of coconuts in a high wind. And second, I liked being alert and protective. Somebody could've come along and tried to feel her up. But not with me there. For all I knew she would wake up so refreshed and grateful she would want to reward me: *Look, Billy, I'm going to put these blankets over me and pretend to go back to sleep. I'll bet you've never felt up a girl before, so go right ahead. Then when you talk about it with the guys, you won't have to sit there and lie.*

"I'll just be a minute," Wes said, turning off the ignition in the parking lot of a Circle K convenience store and bringing me back from Fantasyland.

A couple of girls standing by the phone checked Wes out as he went in. I mean *really* checked him out. No

4

wonder, either. He might have been the best-looking guy I'd ever seen outside of the movies: his jeans were perfect, his white Western shirt was perfect, his boots were perfect. There wasn't a hair out of place. Plus he had broad shoulders, narrow hips, and a killer mustache.

They were too young for him, but he couldn't have cared less anyway. I knew he wasn't into women, but still it really floored me. Girls he could have had just like that, and he didn't care!

They drifted my way, nudging each other and pretending to look at the van, which was perfect, too — four-wheel drive, leather upholstery, tinted windows, stereo. The works.

I wished I'd sat on my suitcase; instead, as they got closer, I casually let my arm droop out the window so they would see my new bracelet. My new masculine bracelet.

Clang. It slipped off and rolled under the car. I climbed out, feeling dizzy for a second, then got down on my hands and knees and showed the girls my butt while I groped around on the sizzling asphalt.

I was still trying to will away my red face when Wes came back. He glanced at my snickering audience.

"It looks better on you," I said, holding out the bracelet.

"Let's trade." He handed me one of the Cokes he was carrying, plus a pair of sunglasses with mirrored lenses. "So you don't go home in September with wrinkles."

I slipped them on. Ah. For the first time I could really see those two girls. Neither of them was exactly dressed for heavy weather, and one of them — the cute one —

had this little belt of perspiration just above her shorts.

They stopped laughing as Wes backed away, and as we pulled out of the lot I gave them a little wave. The cute one waved back.

I relaxed in the seat and sipped my Coke. She'd seemed a little sorry to see me go. I looked at myself in the mirror on my side. Pretty mysterious behind those new glasses, dude. Pretty intriguing.

"With all that curly hair and that white skin, you look like an Irish poet," my uncle said.

"A short Irish poet." I fought back a blush.

"I imagine you do okay," he said calmly.

If he meant what I think he meant, I didn't. I was popular enough, I guess, and my name came up enough, I suppose, when girls were whispering about who liked who. But I hadn't really *done* anything.

That was one of the reasons I wanted to come to Tucson. Sure, it was a learning experience and a chance to travel and a way to work at a racetrack and to see if being a vet appealed to me. But I also wanted to *do* something. Have a real girlfriend, maybe. Or at least meet a girl who also wanted to do something. Or at least wouldn't mind if I did something, and if I did, wouldn't tell the world.

In Bradleyville, everybody knew everybody else's business. In tenth grade, there were about a hundred and fifty kids. We were like a huge family. Everybody already had his own little niche: we knew who the jocks were, we knew who the class president was, we knew which girl would be class secretary because she'd been class secretary every year since sixth grade. We knew who the bad dudes were (we even had a couple of punkers), we knew which girls wanted to get married, which girls wanted to go to college, and which girls did it. Or at least had done it. Once.

And they knew me — Billy Kennedy, the shrimp. Good grades, good outside shooter, fair shortstop, sense of humor, okay guy in general. Virgin.

What I'm getting at is that tucked under the public plans were some private ones of my own for the summer.

"Where's the butts?" I asked as we headed out of the city.

"I beg your pardon."

"Those big things cowboys ride around on."

"Buttes," he said after a moment. "Butts with an *e*. All that cowboy scenery is up north."

Butts. What a moron! Wes didn't say anything until my face stopped glowing. I looked out over miles and miles of nothing but big cactuses, all of them with their hands up like they were being robbed.

"Almost home," he announced, making a wide turn and pulling into Nuevo Grande Estates.

Since I hoped Wes would let me drive sometime, I tried to keep the streets straight. Down Grande to Nuevo, left on Little Grande to Old Nuevo, right on Mucho Grande.

"What's it mean, anyway, Nuevo Grande?"

"New Big."

"New big what?"

"Nothing, but it's the American way, right? If it's new and it's big, it's got to be good."

I shook my head. What a place. Like Wes could read

my mind, he pointed to a dump truck that was spilling out tons of green gravel while an old guy in a pith helmet looked on.

"New lawn," he said. "We've got one just like it, so that'll be one of your chores this summer, to mow the stones."

"You're kidding."

"Yeah."

Then a half-block or so later, we slowed down to let a jogger cross in front of us. He was skinny and dripping sweat.

"Your dad still jog?" Wes asked.

"Every day."

All of a sudden I could see my dad just as clear as anything, leaning in the doorway, back against the frame, panting. He always wanted me to run with him, but I thought my legs were too short. I refused to take three steps to his two. I would've felt like some little pooch trotting along beside his master, but I didn't tell him that. At least not in so many words. He'd say, "Okay, maybe later." And he'd rub my head. That was something he always did. Suddenly I missed him. So I just did it to myself as Wes parked in the driveway and opened the back. But it wasn't the same. It was like kissing the mirror and saying, "Hi, there, tall and handsome." Just not the same as the real thing.

With Wes holding my elbow like I was seven thousand years old, I wobbled up to the front door. As he fumbled with the keys, I leaned against the wall. For an instant. Then my arm started to smoke.

"Is it always this hot?"

8

"Nope."

"Good."

"In July it gets hotter."

What a card. Wes swung the door open and a wall of cool air collapsed on me. *Fantastic!* I staggered in, clutching my throat. I was hamming it up a little, but only a little.

Wes looked around proudly. "Like it?"

Everything was vanilla-colored and clean like you wouldn't believe. There were these great little half-moons of glass set right in the walls. I'd never seen anything like it. But before I could say something complimentary, the phone rang.

"I wonder who that is," he said meaningfully.

I knew what he was getting at. "Don't you have any friends?"

"None with a son who just got off the 3:15 from Kansas City."

He reached for the phone — which was a big Snoopy holding a bone-shaped receiver — and got it on the third ring. "Hello, Loraine," he said without even asking. "He's fine. No, he doesn't look tired." Then he held the phone out to me.

"Hi," I said. "I'm fine. Honest."

"Hi, Cookie." My mom has this great voice, low and husky. She could have been a singer, but she wasn't; she was a nurse. I always thought that people got better faster just by having her talk to them.

"We miss you," she said.

"Yeah, me too."

"Do you like it out there?"

So far I liked the girls and the clothes they didn't wear. But I just said, "It's okay. It's hot."

Then she said, "Walter, don't!" But you could tell she didn't mean it. I guess my dad was fooling around. That's when it hit me that they could get along fine on their own. No Billy to cook for or pick up or take out. No Billy to put in his two cents at the video store or to insist on anchovies at Shakey's.

"Don't rent my room while I'm gone," I blurted.

"Good thing you said something, kiddo. We've got a line of teenage boys outside a block long."

"Well, if you really need the money, okay. But only for three months, and nobody tall."

"Your dad says to tell you he loves you."

"And your mom," Dad said, grabbing the phone, "says the same thing."

"Yeah," I replied, turning so Wes couldn't see me. "Likewise."

Then Dad asked to talk to Wes and I handed him the bone. While they talked I looked around. It was hands down the cleanest place I had ever been in. Everything was perfect, just like Wes's clothes and car. There was lots of glass and polished stuff. It was all Indiany, if you know what I mean. Semi-scary masks on the walls and little statues all over the place. I leaned down to look at one. He was holding a spear in one hand and a gourd or something in the other. I leaned closer.

Holy shit. It was his pecker! I jumped like I'd been goosed. What a thing to have in your living room.

Flustered, I made for a chair, but it was so white and I felt so grungy from the trip that I stopped myself.

"Sit on the sonofabitch," Wes said, putting his hand over the receiver. "When I want you to worship the furniture, I'll tell you."

I was tired and the chair was real soft. Behind me Wes crooned, "Everything's fine. If you send money, I won't spend it. Use it for something you need." I put my head back for just a second.

"Billy," Wes said softly.

"I wasn't asleep."

"Really?" He touched his chin to show me there was something wrong with mine. "Then you're a chronic drooler. Remind me to have you eat over a basin."

I wiped with my forearm. He picked up my stuff and I followed him down the hall. "Here we are," he said, throwing open the door.

Everything was cool as sherbet and, naturally, perfect. There was a painting of a huge pair of lips and right underneath it on the dresser a red sculpture, also lips.

"Shower," Wes said, pointing. "Closets, fabulous view, et cetera." Then he picked up half the sculpture. "Phone."

"I can hardly wait," I said, "to see what the one in the bathroom looks like."

Wes laughed out loud, a big boomer of a laugh. "That's funny," he said. "I like that. We're going to get along all right."

I sat on the edge of the bed, which had been turned back. The sheets were the color of pineapple.

"I'll just sleep a little," I murmured, "and then I'll get up."

"Good plan. Original, too."

Then he was gone and I was alone, really alone for the first time in twenty-seven hours.

As I brushed my teeth — Mom had drilled that into me — I inspected myself in the mirror. Did I look different? More Western? I thought I could see the hint of a tan. Maybe I'd go home dark as mahogany. Maybe the sun would just grab me and pull me up a few inches like it did to plants in those time-lapse movies in Science I. I'd stride off the train in September a different height, a different color, a different person. Ahead of me? A rich and rewarding junior and senior year as basketball star and all-round Great Guy. Behind me? A memorable summer in a quaint Southwestern village where grateful heiresses in abbreviated sunsuits stroked the muzzles of priceless Arabian thoroughbreds I'd miraculously healed.

Then I saw the new pimple on my nose. Right on the end. I scrubbed it with Phiso-derm until it glowed. If Wes peeked in to see if I was okay, I'd look like Rudolph.

I couldn't sleep after that, so I unpacked, found a drawer for my socks, and hung my short-sleeved shirts — all six of them and all with stripes running up and down so I'd look taller — in the closet. Finally I unpacked my books. Just handling them made me feel better. Standing them on the desk all in a row made me feel more at home. I couldn't help but think of my folks. They'd sit at either end of the long, broken-down couch in the living room, both with a book, both with a lamp of their own, both with their legs stretched out and only their feet touching. Then they'd read.

My mom always went barefoot around the house, and

her pink, scrubbed-looking toes would snuggle up against my dad's in his big, thick, white socks. Mom's feet were absolutely still, but Dad's were always moving, always waving a little like stuff does on the bottom of the sea.

Anyway, I read a few pages of one of my new books. It didn't put me to sleep; it was terrific. But the ritual did the trick — holding the soft covers, turning the even softer pages, listening to the smooth sentences lap against my brain.

I put the book down and turned off the light. It wasn't dark outside yet, so I could still see. There were those giant lips. Whose were they, a man's or a woman's? Men kissing each other. Unbelievable. I couldn't get that to make sense at all. The idea made my stomach feel funny.

But I'd felt really comfortable with Wes, right from the beginning. Let's face it, I'd had some doubts. Of course he was my dad's brother, and Dad and I'd had some man-to-man talks about being gay. But still, it wasn't just going to a new place to live for a while with somebody I'd only talked to on the phone and thanked for the presents. It was going somewhere new to live with somebody who was really different from me. Somebody who was homosexual.

Believe me, I hadn't told anybody in Bradleyville High School. They just wouldn't have understood.

When I woke up, part of me was still in some screwy dream where Wes was wearing a blue dress and a big blond wig and my dad was chatting with him like nothing was wrong at all. The other part of me saw the sun still lasering between the drapes and remembered I was in

Tucson, where it was obviously so hot it never even got dark.

I got up then, took a shower, tried to pretend I desperately needed a shave, slipped into a clean shirt and jeans, and made my way toward the kitchen.

Wes had his back to me, talking on the Snoopy phone. He'd changed clothes while I napped: a turquoise shirt replaced the white one, a silver belt where the black one had been. His hair was so smooth it looked like he'd ironed it.

"No," he was saying, "it's just against the law, pure and simple. I'll put one of the lawyers on it, Ted. You concentrate on getting well."

I coughed self-consciously.

"Hi," he said, turning around after he'd hung up. "Breakfast?"

"Breakfast? Uh . . . sure."

"Sunny-side up?"

I nodded and sat down. The napkins were in silver rings. They looked like messages from a long way off.

"Wes," I said, unfolding the white linen, "why are we eating breakfast?"

"It's breakfast time."

"Oh." I fiddled with the heavy silverware. "What time is it?"

"Nine-thirty." He pointed at the clock with his spatula.

"At night?"

He shook his head sadly. "If this damage is permanent, I think we can sue Amtrak."

"It's *day?*"

"Tuesday. You slept from Monday at five till Tuesday

at nine-thirty. Sixteen and a half hours. I figure if this keeps up you'll be a cinch to have around this summer."

"Hey, I'm supposed to start work on Tuesday!"

"Relax. I called Jack and explained."

"He won't think I'm lazy, will he?"

"Those horses aren't going anywhere. You and I'll have a day off; I'll show you around."

He slid a warm plate in front of me. The eggs were — what else? — perfect. When I cooked at home, the yolks always broke, then fried real hard. But Wes's beamed up at me just like in a restaurant.

I wanted to ask him if he could cook because he was gay or if he was gay because he could cook. But that seemed stupid, barely a notch above "Hey, so how's it feel to be queer, huh?"

Dad had said to just be cool about it.

As we drove toward Tucson, I tried to get my bearings, still hoping Wes would want me to drive and I could find my way home without asking, thereby demonstrating my cleverness and dependability. But everything looked pretty much the same: desert, low adobe-looking houses, and cactuses (cacti, I guess). Not like home, where some of the houses had names of their own: the Simpson house, the old Fiscus place, Willoughby's.

"Road runner," said Wes, pointing to a bird about a foot and a half long, which darted off when we got close.

"You're kidding!" I turned around in the seat and tried to find him in the brush. "I love those cartoons." Just then another one streaked across the road in front of us. "What do they eat?"

"Plenty. Lizards, little snakes, birds' eggs."

"I don't see any snakes or birds."

"They're there, all right," he assured me, shifting into second gear to climb the last hundred yards, then stopping at the top of a little hill.

"Nice view, huh?"

"If you're into sand."

"I didn't know who the hell I was," he said mildly, "until I came to the desert. It'll do that, bring you right up out of yourself and shine the light in your eyes."

Did he mean being gay? I decided not to ask, not yet, anyway.

Pretty soon there were enormous billboards for some local attractions: movie sets, caves with outlaw gold, that sort of thing. Each advertisement was like a big window into the West I'd imagined: colorful scenery, black stallions, desperadoes. The funny thing was that the *real* West was all around me, miles and miles of it.

"Look at this," Wes said happily as we cruised down Fourth Avenue. "Every parking space is full."

"You like that?"

"If they're all shopping in my place I do."

We roamed around one block, then another before Wes pulled into a space. "You don't mind walking, do you?"

I looked up at the sky. Not a cloud anywhere. "Wait a minute, okay? I don't want the whole world to see this." Then I fumbled under the seat for the sunblock I'd smuggled on board. Wes watched me trowel it on. "It's Mom's idea," I explained, reaching for my hat.

"And that keeps your hair from getting sunburned?"

"I promised," I said losing another battle of the blush.

We walked for a dozen yards or so, then I stopped.

"What's wrong, kiddo?"

"Do I look stupid with all this stuff on me?"

He put his hand on my shoulder, careful not to get grease all over him. "You're fine," he said sincerely. "And, anyway, a promise is a promise."

Wes's shop was as elegant as everything else he owned or wore or drove. While he talked with one of the clerks, I prowled around checking out the stacks of blankets and rugs, staring through the shiny cases at the bracelets, rings, and knives. I was afraid I'd drop anything I touched, so I kept my hands on my hat, holding it awkwardly first in front, then behind me like a shy nudist.

Then, when Wes was explaining something about Bisbee turquoise to a customer and I was leaning on a display case full of belt buckles nearby, the bell over the door jangled and a woman came in pushing someone in a wheelchair. She had a lot of gray in her long ponytail, and her T-shirt featured a large clenched fist. The guy in the chair was as shiny with lotion as I was, but he wore a real cowboy hat, even if it was too big for him.

"Wes!" she said. "Hi."

"Suzette. Hang on a minute."

He turned away, finished his conversation, then hurried toward us. "Billy," he said. "I want you to meet somebody. Fifteen years ago Suzette and I were going to change the world."

"And we did, all right." She held out her hand for me

17

to shake. Then she turned to my uncle. "You know Michael. He lived here in the seventies." Suzette tilted the hat back so Wes could see.

"You were at the Stonewall march, weren't you?" asked Wes.

"Right up in front."

"Sure, I remember. How are you?"

"I always liked Tucson," Michael said, pausing to catch his breath. "So I thought I'd come back for a while."

Nobody said anything for a few seconds. I looked from Wes to Michael to Suzette and back again. There was something going on, but I didn't know what it was.

"Well," Michael wheezed. "We've got lots to do."

"We're going too, right, Billy?"

"Sure."

Outside we said goodbye again, then took off in opposite directions. We'd only walked half a block when Wes handed me the keys.

"You drive, okay?"

"Really?"

"Really."

A few minutes later I sat in the driver's seat and adjusted everything. You'd have thought I was setting out on a round-the-world trip sponsored by Arco.

I sure love to drive. Mom never lets me because she sees too many kids brought into the hospital where she works, but Dad does. Sometimes. That's a secret, but what isn't a secret is my not being able to use the car by myself until I'm eighteen. Mom had put her foot down.

I kept my enthusiasm to myself, though, because Wes

had gone moody on me. While he stared out the window, I imagined how tall I looked perched in that leather bucket seat.

"Jesus, I used to work out with that guy," Wes blurted. "I didn't even recognize him at first."

"Michael's really sick, isn't he?"

"He's dying, Billy."

I looked at the speedometer. *Dying.*

"He's dying of AIDS."

And I'd shaken that guy's hand.

"You don't get it that way," he said, reading my mind again.

I blushed. "I didn't mean to . . ."

"It's okay. I know you didn't." Then he sighed.

"I've just never seen anybody like that before," I explained.

"I have, but I never get used to it." He shook his head. "I don't see how Suzette does it. I can handle anything on the phone, but . . ."

"Do you talk to sick people on the phone?"

"Well, they're not all sick. Remember that guy this morning? Ted had just been diagnosed, so he got fired. And that's still against the law, so we'll go to court and get his job back."

"*Still* against the law?"

"Laws can be changed. There are some people who want AIDS victims to wear ID bracelets or get tattoos. And then there are the ones who think in terms of concentration camps." Just then his hand shot toward the wheel. "Watch out!"

Ahead of me a woman in a station wagon had stopped

to drop her kid off. I slammed on the brakes, and the van skidded for a few yards. We were just inches from her back window and her dog was barking like crazy.

"Sorry," I said, easing over to the curb. "Maybe you should drive?"

"You were doing fine until I started giving my speech." He pointed toward the next stoplight. "Left there and we're almost home."

"Okay." But I didn't take the van out of park.

"What's wrong?" Wes asked.

"I guess I'm wondering if you're okay."

"What?"

I repeated it, louder this time.

His voice got a little hard. "You wouldn't be here if I had AIDS, Billy."

"It wasn't me I was worried about," I said, nervously wiping off the spotless dashboard with my hand. "I meant," and I looked right at him then, "are *you* okay."

It was his turn to look. For a few seconds it was intense, like he was trying to see inside me. Then he relaxed and even smiled a little.

"Yes," he said. "Thanks for asking."

2

"How did you get to know a horse trainer, anyway?" I asked as Wes drove me to work next morning.

"He comes in the shop and buys jewelry for his girl-friends."

"And you just happened to mention that you had a nephew who wanted a job?"

"Something like that."

We made a sweeping turn off Fourth Avenue and picked up River Road. There were the first billboards for Sunset Downs. Twilight Racing, they said. Huge horses rushed toward us, their teeth bared.

"Do you ever go?" I asked.

"To the track? I've been, but I'm a terrible gambler. How about you?"

"I promised to save what I make this summer for college."

He pulled up to a guard's shack and asked for Jack Ferguson; then we parked by one of the sheds.

I wrinkled my nose. "It smells back here."

"Horse crap. Or did they skip that part in the veterinarian's brochure?"

I was beginning to feel a little wary. The place was hot and dusty and needed paint.

"This isn't exactly what I imagined," I confessed.

"What'd you expect?"

"I thought I'd at least be working inside." Where was the spotless waiting room with its ferns and fish tanks? Where was the nurse with the curl peeking out from under her starched cap, the same nurse whose uniform wouldn't stay buttoned at the top?

"Wait and see," advised Wes.

"This Mr. Ferguson didn't say what I'd be doing?"

"Nope. I was talking to your dad on the phone. He said you wanted to work with animals. Horses are animals, and Jack just happened to be in the shop."

I watched some horses plod by. They looked like they'd been pulling plows. This was nothing like ABC's coverage of the Kentucky Derby.

"What made you want to be a vet, anyway?" Wes asked.

"I don't know exactly, but I always have. Even when I was a little kid and everybody else played doctor, I was always a vet."

"You show me your puppy, I'll show you mine."

I tried not to blush and almost succeeded. "We'd just get all the kids' pets together and I'd fix them up. Of course they were always well to start with, so I looked pretty good."

"Your dad really got hot for the idea. And since he was telling me about it and Jack was there bitching about how good help was hard to get . . . well, one thing just led to another and here we are."

I looked around. "Yeah," I said dubiously.

"I think your dad would really like to see you make about eighty thousand a year."

"My dad?"

"Just while we were chatting I got the idea that he wanted something better for you than teaching."

"Gee, he loves teaching."

"I know, but he doesn't love worrying about bills. I think he was relieved when you talked about doing something where you could make a ton of money."

Great. Now I also had to worry about disappointing my dad!

Just then something scared one of the horses, and the guy who was leading him, a guy who looked like he picked his teeth with a switchblade, got dragged about six yards before he took charge again.

"Never a dull moment," Wes said.

I hadn't been around a real horse in I don't know how long. They were huge. And dangerous. How did you take care of a sick horse, anyway? They didn't exactly seem like good patients.

Just then three or four more came by. They had riders this time. Girl riders, and they all had their names burned into their leather chaps: June, Cindy, Bev, Cara Mae.

Wes and I watched two older guys, both of them drinking those little cartons of milk, hurry past the guard and right up to the girls.

"You went too fast, Whitney," snapped one of them.

"She was running on her own."

"Yeah? Well, she got tired as hell the last eighth."

"Isn't that what a workout's for?"

"Why don't you just ride and I'll do the training, okay?"

The blonde — her chaps said Cara Mae — just shrugged; then she looked at us (at me) and smiled. I watched her ride away. Not one of them had anything more on top than thin old T-shirts with the sleeves hacked off. Their arms were strong and brown. Tucked in the backs of their skintight jeans were springy-looking whips and their hair was hidden under beat-up helmets with leather chin straps.

"Pretty cute," said Wes.

"I, uh, was looking at the horse."

"I'll believe that when you ask it to go to the movies." Then he waved and took a step or two. "Here comes Jack now."

"Is this the entire trainer or just the part that hires?" I asked.

Wes laughed. "He used to be a jockey. He's a little sensitive about his height, so be advised."

"I can relate to that."

They shook hands, then Wes introduced me. Mr. Ferguson was wiry and tanned. And, God bless him, he was about half a head shorter than me. In fact, about every third person I saw around Sunset Downs was short. Maybe it wouldn't be such a bad place after all.

"Call me at the shop just before you're done," said Wes, giving me an encouraging pat, "and I'll come and get you."

I nodded, and Mr. Ferguson said, "Follow me."

We walked along without saying anything, cutting between barns, dodging big piles of smelly straw. One thing

I could see for sure: everybody believed in luck. On the bleached-out awnings were four-leaf clovers and horseshoes and giant 7's. Nailed to the top halves of the Dutch doors of every stall were big initials — of the trainer, I guessed — and even on the clothes that'd been hung out in the sun to dry. Either people were proud of themselves or somebody would steal your sandwich if it didn't have your name on it.

"Mr. Ferguson, is everything monogrammed back here?"

"Call me Jack. And, yeah, everything but the horses."

"They're branded," I said, glad to know something.

"Nope." Without slowing down even a little, he pulled out his lower lip. "Tattooed with a number inside here."

"Oh, yeah. That's right," I said, as if it had just slipped my mind.

We'd only walked for a couple of minutes, but the scenery changed fast. Nothing had looked too great to begin with, but it went downhill from there. There weren't any real flowers like there had been before, just droopy plastic ones. The awnings weren't just shabby; the sun and wind had torn them loose.

Jack stopped right beside a cactus with gray-looking underpants hanging off it like some kind of weird fruit. His barns didn't look any worse than the ones around it, but that isn't saying much. Everything needed paint or nails or something. Encouragement at the very least.

He turned and faced me. "Let me tell you what's what around here, Billy, so we don't have to spend a lot of time blowin' in each other's ear, agreed?"

"Yes, sir."

"I'm in Tucson because I couldn't catch on anywhere else, anyways not the way I wanted. I went to the East Coast and tried Belmont; I went to the West Coast and tried Santa Anita. Nothin' doin'. I was either unlucky or not good enough. I don't know which and I don't want to think about it, follow me?"

"I think so."

"Now, your job is to make my job easier. Be here when I say, do what I tell you to when I tell you. And for that you get to work long hours for goddamn little pay."

"Sounds great so far."

He didn't bother to laugh. "Now I want this summer to work out, but if it don't, I'll fire your butt just like that, and then I'll be mad at your uncle." He took off his battered hat and wiped his forehead with a red kerchief. And when he did, his hair moved. All of it.

"And I don't want to be mad at your uncle. And stop staring at my hairpiece. That's my problem. Wes don't care about my rug any more than I care what he does when the bars close, understand?"

"Yes, sir."

"And I ain't no goddamn liberal, either."

"Yes, sir."

"He's always been square with me, that's all. We've always got along. Thanks to your uncle, lots of happy ladies wearin' Zuni inlay right now."

The two thousand wrinkles around his eyes relaxed and unfanned a little when he thought of all those happy ladies.

"Understand?" He held out his right hand. "Agreed?"

26

"Sure," I said, shaking it, impressed by the strength of his grip.

"Then I'll get Lew and he can show you the ropes."

I stepped into some shade. He'd made me sweat. The sunblock was running off in little rivers. Then Jack walked out of a back room with Lew and I got even more nervous. Lew looked like the kind of kid I'd seen on TV shows about the streets of L.A. and New York: six feet tall, paratrooper boots, fatigue pants, ripped T-shirt, an earring with a skull on it. But he wasn't one of those emaciated punks who look like they need about three years of home cooking. He was in good shape, with the kind of arms I always wanted, except that if I had his, my hands would drag on the ground.

Jack introduced us. I waited to see if Lew wanted to shake hands. Instead he put on his shades. That was cool. I put on my shades. Then we looked at each other. He wasn't really a punk at all; he seemed more the combat-crazed type.

"You know what to do, Lew," Jack said. "I'll be in the office."

"Let's go, Short Stuff," Lew snapped.

I didn't budge. Maybe I'd always be Short Stuff in Bradleyville, but I wasn't going to be Short Stuff all across the nation.

"Name's Billy," I said, swallowing hard and mentally replaying all the Clint Eastwood movies I'd ever seen.

Lew glared at me from under his crewcut, which was bleached out white as a towel. "Oh, yeah? Suppose I want to call you Short Stuff. What are you going to do about it?"

"Maybe I'll call you something back."

"Like what, Runt?"

"Like Blockhead."

"Oh, yeah, Shrimp?"

"Yeah, Buttface."

Then we stared at each other. Lew stared down. I stared up. At least I stood there, and all of a sudden it was over.

"So," he said with a shrug, "your name is Billy. B.F.D. Let's go, kid."

I was so relieved I let the *kid* go. I was just sixteen, right? In a way, I was a kid. In a way, it wasn't really an insult.

I followed Lew past stall after stall. Every now and then he'd put out his hand — the one without the glove — and pat one of the horses, who stared at us like convicts. So I reached out, too.

"Not that one," he said. "That's Buckskin. He don't like to be touched."

"How can you tell them apart? They all look the same."

"They're different, believe me."

As he rinsed out a couple of buckets, I peered into the nearest stall. Inside, a horse was standing with its front feet in tubs of ice water.

"What's wrong with him?" I asked.

"Her." Then he handed me a couple of buckets. "Know which end to put the feed in?"

"The one with the teeth?"

"So do it."

"Which ones bite and which ones don't?" I asked.

"You'll find out."

It didn't take me long to see that Lew was right. They were all different, and not just different colors, either, but personalities too — shy, curious, friendly, angry.

"The one called Soldier Returns is lying down," I said, making my third trip with the heavy buckets. "Should I get her up?"

"Did I tell you to leave 'em alone if they're resting?"

"No."

"Maybe you aren't hopeless, after all."

"Thanks."

"That one over there, that's Moon's Medicine. You won't find her lying down. She's a stall walker," Lew said, hosing out the wheelbarrow.

"What's that?" I was glad for an excuse to stop for a minute. It wasn't even ten o'clock and I was tired.

"Just a nervous type that can't quiet down. They're not worth shit."

"To who?"

"To Jack. Or to you and me when we bet. She uses it all up pacing around and there's nothing left for the race."

"Why does Jack keep her?"

"Not up to Jack. He just trains what his owners give him."

Boy, there was a lot to learn.

"How long have you been doing this, Lew?"

"Since six this morning."

"I mean —"

"Oh. Three years, since I was fifteen."

"Do you like it?"

"I like to get paid, and Jack's watching. Let's get to work."

It *was* work, too, cleaning out every stall, putting in fresh straw, and carting the old stuff out back. The biggest shock to me was how heavy horse manure is. My back started to ache after fifteen minutes, then my legs and arms.

"What happens to this stuff now?" I asked Lew, passing him with my wheelbarrow piled to the sky.

"Mushroom guys pick it up."

"Mushroom guys?" I pictured little short men with big hats.

"For the mushroom farm," he said. "They grow in this stuff."

"A piece of information," I shouted back, "that changes my mind about salads forever."

It was almost noon before we finished; I felt like I'd sweated away five pounds.

"Your turn," Lew said as we got close to the office, "to go and get sandwiches."

"Why is it my turn? You never took one."

"I went yesterday."

"I wasn't here yesterday."

"Shit, okay. We flip for it."

I called heads and lost, but I'd stood my ground, so I felt pretty good as I hunted for the cafeteria. It wasn't much past noon, but the backstretch, which had been so busy with people and horses and pickup trucks, was almost deserted.

The mean guard dogs were asleep. So were the skinny

cats that'd been all over the place. I passed a goat tethered to the door of a dim stall. He was asleep, too, just like the one lonely duck with her bill tucked under her wing sitting in the dust and dreaming, probably, about lagoons.

Everybody I passed nodded at me or touched their hats or both. People seemed pretty friendly, really, even if they did — most of them, anyway — look a little rough around the edges. It was hands down the most Western place I'd seen yet. Nothing like modern Tucson with its shiny buildings or Nuevo Grande and those stone lawns. On the backstretch most everybody wore boots and hats and jeans and big belt buckles. And lots of people rode horses.

As I stood in line for sandwiches, I looked down at my Air Jordans — the ones I'd been so proud of a week ago — and at my sweaty striped shirt. Everybody else looked like a cowboy. I looked like a high school kid in a funny hat.

Lew and Jack and I were sitting outside the office eating when the blonde girl I'd seen that morning, the one named Cara Mae, rode up, leaned forward in the stirrups a time or two, then hooked one long leg over the saddle horn.

Nobody said anything, but there was something going on. My folks always talked about vibes, like good vibes or bad vibes. These were jittery vibes.

I smiled up at her and, like a numbnuts, waved the hand with the sandwich in it. She had a big, eager smile.

"Hi," she said to me. "Hi, Lew. Hi, Mr. Ferguson."

Lew gave the coolest of nods. Nothing from Jack.

"I saw in the overnights you're gonna run Moon's Medicine Saturday," she said. "I was thinkin' she might need to go three furlongs tomorrow or the next day and wondering if you'd put me on her."

Cara Mae had that look that you get while you watch your speech teacher finish her notes about you.

"Sweetheart," Jack said, looking up from his boots for the first time, "I'm not about to forget that little filly who paid three-twenty to win when I should of got twelve or fourteen bucks. Now I've told you before, and I'll . . ."

She didn't let him finish, jerking on the reins so hard her horse's eyes flew open. "Aw, the hell with you," she yelled. Then she was gone, literally in a cloud of dust.

Jack waved it away, turning his head to keep the grit out of his eyes. "She can ride some," he said absently, "but she is a handful."

I glanced at Lew. If I thought he was about to add to the saga, I was wrong.

"You want that?" he asked, eyeing the rest of my sandwich.

"Yeah, as a matter of fact."

"Hey, just asking."

"Knock it off," Jack said mildly as he stood up, yawned, and stretched. "Let's settle something here." He looked at Lew. "No bullshit now — how'd Billy do today?"

"Okay," Lew said after a second. Then, "Not bad."

"You guys can work together, then, you get along?"

I waited for Lew to say it first.

"Sure," he said, then I said it, too.

"Good. So, you know the routine now, Billy, just get here earlier. Can you do that?"

"I'll have to ask Uncle Wes. I think so."

"And I'll need you both this Saturday night for the sixth race."

"We haven't got a prayer," said Lew.

Jack shrugged. "Hell of a lot less with her just walking around the goddamn stall." Then he yawned again, took off his hat, took off his toupee, and scratched his head. "I'm beat. I'll see you boys tomorrow."

"Can I use the phone?" I asked. "I need a ride home."

"Where's home?" Lew wanted to know. When I told him, he said, "Forget it. I'll take you. Let me get my stuff."

I sat by myself for a minute or two, staring at the space where Cara Mae had been. What was I doing thinking about her? I'd only seen her on a horse, but she was probably taller than me, anyway.

When Lew came back, the first thing out of my mouth was, "What's the story with that blonde girl?"

"Whitney? Forget it."

"Why was Jack mad?"

"Oh, he had this little filly named Hurry Up that he was kind of hiding from everybody."

I shook my head to show I didn't understand.

"You know, working her out real slow, using some big fat exercise girl, anything so she don't look all that good to the crowd."

"Cara Mae's not fat."

"No shit, Sherlock. But Jack hires her 'cause Cara

Mae's kind of pitiful sometimes. Tells her to go an easy four furlongs and that's all."

"Is that what she does — exercise horses?"

"Yeah, free-lance type. Anyway, that day she's got her back up about something, because she gets that filly onto the track, sits right down on her, and they go forty-six and change."

"Is that fast?"

"It is for what Jack wanted."

"So then everybody caught on that she was a faster horse than she'd looked."

"Now you got the picture. Man, they bet with both hands the day she ran."

"But she won."

"Sure, but her odds were so low it wasn't worth betting."

I didn't understand that part of it yet, but instead of asking I heard myself say, "I think she's cute."

"Whitney? Did you see the tits on her?"

"No."

"That's because she hasn't got any." Then he lifted me off the bench by my upper arm like teachers in grade school used to.

"Come with me, kid. I'll show you cute."

I followed his eyes to a big copper-colored Cadillac that was oozing our way. It had — I'm serious — steer horns for a hood ornament. Lew waved, and a hand with a lot of nail polish on it waved back.

"That's Abby Dayton," he half whispered. "Her old man owns the best horses on the grounds and votes

Republican with his eyes closed. It makes him nuts that Abby goes out with me." He waved jauntily as she stopped and turned off the engine. "Let me get her out of the car so you can see her body. It is choice."

"That's okay," I said. "I can tell she's cute."

He'd already walked over to the window on the driver's side and was leaning in, propping himself so his muscles popped out. Abby was already stroking his forearm.

"Get on out here," I heard him say. "I told Billy you had the cutest behind in Arizona."

"Lew Coley, you are bad," she said with a *tsk-tsk* in her voice, but I also noticed she hopped right out and stood with her back to me. She looked like one of the girls on the feed and grain calendar in Jack's office — incredibly curvy, huge cowboy hat with feathers in the band, big hand-tooled belt with her name on the back, shiny boots made out of some sort of lizard.

Lew put his arms around her, and, looking at me over her shoulder, pointed at her bottom. Naturally, I blushed. Then he introduced us.

"You're cute," she said. And I blushed again. "And sweet, too. My, I haven't seen a man blush since Terry Stuart peed his new jeans at the FFA Rodeo in Sonoita when I was nine."

"I'm just sunburned," I said, pointing to the sky.

"I don't see how," Lew commented, "between the goose grease you use and that wonderful hat."

"Gimme a break, okay?"

"Billy's got the hots for Cara Mae," Lew announced.

"Good for him. She could use a nice boyfriend."

"I don't either have the . . ." but Lew didn't let me finish.

"She needs more than a boyfriend. She needs a complete overhaul."

"So she's a little moody. You can get past that, can't you, Billy?"

"Abby!" someone shouted from about a block away. She rolled her eyes. "Daddy." She turned to Lew. "Tell me something pessimistic," she said cheerfully.

"Better live for today," Lew warned her, "for tomorrow we may die."

She stamped her foot and gave a little enthusiastic wiggle. "God, I love that!"

"Abby!" bellowed her father, and this time she got in the car.

We watched her back the Caddy all the way to where her dad was fuming. Then Lew and I walked toward the parking lot.

"This is it," he said, climbing in.

"A jeep. Cool!"

"Not just cool. Necessary."

"How's that?" I asked innocently.

"I'm not just trying to get into Abby's pants. I mean it about there not being any tomorrow."

I looked over at him. He was half smiling.

"The big cities go first, see, but I'm in my jeep heading for the mountains." He gestured with his crewcut toward the Santa Catalinas. "By the time the radioactivity gets here or the troops or whatever, I'm holed up with a lot of food, bottled water, videos, books, and a few dozen other people who knew the score all along, too. Not to mention their grateful daughters."

"You're kidding."

"Am I?" He started the jeep, popping the clutch and throwing me back in my seat.

3

"So it's been a hard week, but you like it," Wes said as I walked into the living room, carefully holding a plate under the huge tuna sandwich he'd fixed for my dinner.

"Yeah, a lot. It's pretty interesting. There's a lot more to it than you'd think."

"Like what?" he asked a little absently. He was hunkered down on the living-room floor inspecting some stuff for the shop: long rugs with zigzag patterns; baskets of all sizes and kinds; a few fertility statues, all with you-know-what in one hand; necklaces, bracelets, rings.

"Oh, which horse to run when."

"Aren't they all pretty much the same?"

"That's what I thought, but actually they're not. Some are way better than others. Jack says his job is to put the right horse in the right race but not make it obvious."

"Why's that?"

"So when he bets he'll win more."

"I know old Jack loves to gamble." Wes inspected another basket critically and set it to one side. "Have you made any miraculous cures yet?"

"All the vets do so far is come back to the barn, look at the horses, shake their heads, and give them shots."

"Maybe you want to be a trainer instead."

"Maybe," I replied, meaning I'd been at the track four days and already changed my career plans nine times.

"And what's so important about tonight?"

"I've never taken a horse to the receiving barn and the saddling paddock before, that's all."

"So this isn't the big race or anything."

"Uh-uh. Moon's Medicine is pretty cheap."

"But there is a big race, isn't there?"

"Labor Day night, last night of the meet." The first of September seemed a light-year away. As far away as being twenty-one.

Just then the doorbell rang. "It's probably Lew," I said.

Wes stood up to say hi, brushing off his spotless linen slacks. If he thought anything about Lew's usual getup, he didn't say it.

"Is all this stuff real?" Lew asked, tiptoeing around the display in his combat boots.

"Real as in made by a Navajo or real as in really imported from Taiwan?"

"I'll bet there's a lot of that phony stuff," Lew said, as if he'd suspected it for a long time.

"It's not all bad. They can computer-program in the flaws if they want to bother."

"Do you sell that, too?"

"Sure, but I don't tell people it's something it's not."

"What flaws," I asked, "can they program in?"

He looked at the blankets all around him, then pointed to a beautiful red one. "The place," he said, "where the spirit can come and go." His voice got quieter as he explained. "Or sometimes it's where the artist was thinking about something else for a second."

"Does that ruin it?"

"Not for me," he said. "And some collectors insist on it. I've seen great mistakes." His face brightened. "A couple of years ago in Santa Fe I saw this rug and my heart started to go boom, boom, boom. It had this one little place, just off from the center. Anybody could see it, and the man who owned the rug didn't know what he had. He just thought it wasn't perfect.

"So I bought it," he went on softly, "and then drove up to see the woman who made it, Mildred Sky. She lived about fifteen miles out of the old part of Santa Fe. And she said that, yes, she'd been weaving when her nephew died."

"And she was right at that spot?"

He nodded. "She told me that something touched her hand. And she knew immediately what it was and she knew what it meant, but there wasn't anything she could do about it right at that moment so she just kept weaving."

"Was her nephew in the same house or something?"

"No, he died in Flagstaff."

"Radical," said Lew.

"If you like anything," Wes added a second or two later and in his normal voice, "you can have it for what it cost me."

"Too bad I'm broke. Abby goes for this stuff," Lew

said, squatting down to pick through the silver bracelets. As he turned, I saw the mushroom-shaped cloud he'd drawn on the back of his T-shirt with a felt tip.

Lew drove for a mile or two with his eyes scrunched up like he was staring into the sun, but it was setting behind us.

"You know what I just remembered," he said. "Your uncle's queer. I've seen his picture in the paper: speaker this, discussion leader that."

"Gay," I said, a little sharply. "Not queer."

"Yeah, whatever. The thing is — you've got a gay uncle. What does that make you?"

"His nephew," I said evenly.

Lew drove for a block or so. Then he grinned and rolled his eyes. "The world's really an amazing place. I'll be sorry to see it go."

"Who says it's going anywhere?"

"My old man, for one."

"So, you've got a gloomy old man. What does that make you?"

Lew smirked, then licked his index finger and made a mark in the air to show I'd scored. "At least he's got a plan to cure AIDS and cancer and all that stuff."

"Which is?"

"Total annihilation. He says that's the up-side of thermonuclear war."

"Mr. Silver Lining."

"You got any money?" he asked abruptly.

"Couple of dollars."

"Let's swing by my house, okay? We got time."

"What's going on?"

"Nothing. Why?"

"You've got this screwy look on your face."

"Relax. Don't be so paranoid. I just want you to meet my folks."

Lew lived just off Prince Road, not ten minutes from the track, in a subdivision called Hacienda Heights which was located, naturally, in one of the lowest parts of the city. In the Heights you looked up to everything. All the houses had tile roofs and fireplaces, but the place hadn't caught on. Half-finished houses stood only a few blocks from places that had really been lived in. Almost everybody had a camper in his driveway except for Lew's dad, who sported a second jeep and a greenish three-quarter-ton truck with a canvas top.

"Take it slow," Lew cautioned as we hopped out.

"Why?"

But Lew had slipped around to one side of the house and then the other, flattened to the wall like a shadow.

"All clear," he hissed.

"All clear for what?"

"Shhhhh."

Inside the stereo was blasting, something about thunder and lightning, I think, and then, "The way you love me is frightening." Lew motioned me on, peering warily into every room.

I didn't have a clue.

"Base camp," he said, hauling me through the kitchen door.

A woman stood at the sink tearing lettuce and smoking a joint. The whole place smelled like a senior class party. She had a perfectly round hairdo, like an Afro, but she was white and so was a lot of her hair. Or at least it was gray. I got a peculiar impulse to blow on it, like a dandelion, and she'd be bald just like that.

Lew walked over, touched a dial on the wall, and cut the sound to nothing. She turned around in slow motion.

"Hi, Mom," Lew said.

"I thought you were at the track."

"Came back for some money."

"As the great Ray Charles said, 'I'm busted.' "

Lew shook his head. "That's cool." Then he introduced me.

"Hi, Billy," she said with a weak smile.

She seemed nice, but she looked a little sad. Just then Lew put his finger to his lips and slipped behind the door.

"What?" I asked, spreading my hands helplessly.

Just as he motioned me to be quiet, the screen door burst open. A man with a machine gun dove through and rolled to his feet. My hands shot up in the air.

"Hand over your squirrel meat," he shouted, "and all edible pupa."

I was trying not to wet my pants. "Lew! Jesus Christ, Lew!"

Right on cue he stepped out, karate-chopped the guy, and wrenched the weapon free. "That'll be ten bucks," he said calmly.

"You earned it," said the robber as he dug into his fatigue pants and handed over the money. He'd shaved his head, then painted it and his face green and gray and black, like a jeep.

"You can put your hands down, Billy," Lew said. "Edgar pays me if I get to him before he gets to me."

"Edgar? This is your dad?"

"Billy Kennedy," Lew said to his father like we'd just met at a cocktail party. "We work together."

"Can you name Primary Targets, Secondary Targets, and draw from memory Fallout Patterns following the strike?" barked Mr. Coley.

"Are you kidding?" I replied, taking a step or two back. But Lew could, and he rattled them off as I looked at his mom, still humming to herself and washing lettuce.

"Another quiz for five bucks, okay?" said Lew. "I'm still a little short."

"Name the contents," his dad snapped, "of the Sanitation Kit necessary for split-second evacuation."

Lew spat out the list: "Portable toilet, three packages disposable toilet bags, one can chlorine bathroom cleanser." Then he grinned. "That'll be a fin. We gotta go."

"Ah," his father whined, "come and look at the Bugoutmobile. It's almost done."

"Well, okay." Lew pocketed the money. "But just for a minute."

Most of the backyard was taken up by a welding rig, a van chassis, and stacked steel slabs, about half of them fastened to the heavy rollbars. I could picture the rest. It'd eventually look like an iron tepee.

"No room for you, Billy," Mr. Coley said calmly. "So when the time comes, just seal yourself in the bathroom with towels and duct tape, okay?"

"You bet."

"Really. You'll remember now?"

I could see his concern through the wavy makeup. "Yes, sir."

"Awesome machine, Edgar. But we've got a horse in the sixth."

I led the way out, calmly opening the wooden gate.

"Don't ever," shouted Mr. Coley, so loud that I jumped about a foot, "just walk through an entrance like that. Throw a bone through first. See if the mutants leap on it."

"Mutants?" I asked. "If there really were mutants, Mr. Coley, wouldn't they be inside eating the disposable toilet bags?"

His dad glowered, but Lew laughed and held out his palm for me to slap.

"Amazing," I said, slipping out the door.

"Let's take the truck," Lew said. But when we climbed in he just sat with his hands on the wheel for a few seconds.

"You're from the old Show-Me state, so I thought I'd show you. Ever seen anything like that before?"

"Uh-uh."

"Lawyer by day, Captain Survival by night."

"They let him in court looking like that?"

"You know what a class action suit is?"

"No."

"Good. That's what he does, the research, anyway.

45

They've got some jerk with a suit to go to court."

I looked at the last bit of the sun, pink like the rind of a Florida grapefruit.

"How'd your dad get into this combat stuff, anyway?"

"He works out with those survivalist types down at the Nautilus on Rincon and Sixth. They teach him this stuff and he practices on me. He had us out in the wilds one time for about a month with nothing but a couple matches and a nail file."

"Doesn't it drive your mom crazy?"

"Obviously." Lew shook his head as he started the truck. "But what the hell. It keeps him in shape and he's not hurting anybody, right?"

"I guess," I said, trying to sound sincere.

He pounded the steering wheel with his fist. "So let's go win a horse race while there is one."

Moon's Medicine would quiet down when there was somebody in the stall with her, so while Lew went to get Jack I kept the nervous horse company. She bumped at me with her big soft nose; I rubbed her absently while I thought about Lew's folks. My mom didn't have to get loaded to make a salad. My dad just ran for exercise. He didn't dress up like foliage and bust down doors.

Was it the Southwest, I wondered? Bradleyville seemed like Normaltown, U.S.A., compared to Tucson. But then in Bradleyville most people thought gay men were diseased Commies, and here my uncle got his picture in the paper.

"Howdy," somebody said, and I turned around to see two guys leaning into the stall. "Fletcher Denman," said the rangy one, offering a hand to shake. "This is Grif."

Grif was a good name for his pal, though anything with one syllable would have been okay. Thor, for example. He was fat, but solid-looking fat. He wore a big leather apron and carried a huge pair of tongs. He looked like a Viking who was down on his luck.

"We're friends of Jack's," Fletcher said, smoothing the brim of his cowboy hat with two hands. "He thinks the world of you, kid."

"Jack does?"

"Says you've got a real way with horses."

"I do?"

"Like with this old hide." He nodded at Moon's Medicine.

"Shoot," I said modestly. "All I do is keep her stall clean and feed her."

"She still roamin' around in here day and night?"

"Day and night," I echoed, shaking my head sympathetically right along with my new friends.

"Billy!"

"Hi, Jack. I was just talking to your —"

"I heard the tail end of it, and don't say no more."

"What are you mad at?" Fletcher and Grif had stepped back a yard or two. They were both grinning, but not nice grins and not at me or Lew, who'd walked in with Jack and was leaning on the horse, taking it all in.

"What'd you tell these pecker-checkers?" Jack demanded.

"He told us," Fletcher said, "this old horse can't win tonight, that's what he told us, didn't you, boy."

"Hey, I'm not your boy."

47

"Goddammit, Billy!" Jack swore at me, then turned to the other two. "You get out of here and leave my help alone."

"See you, Jack," Fletcher said, tipping his hat. "But it won't be in the winner's circle."

"What the hell's the matter with you?" Jack snapped the second they were out of sight.

"They said they were friends of yours."

"And you believed them?"

"Jesus, Jack, how was I supposed to know."

"Don't ever tell nobody nothing about a horse, you understand? Never. I'm trying to make a living back here, goddammit, and I can't do it if I don't bet and I can't get the kind of odds I want if you get on the goddamn public address system and tell the world what I'm doing with my stock."

"Were you going to bet tonight?" I looked at Moon's Medicine, whose chin was almost dragging in the straw. "On her?"

"That ain't the point, Billy. I want people to bet tonight because she isn't liable to run. Next time I might have figured something out and then I don't want 'em all over her, understand?"

"I guess," I said, but I didn't, not really. "Anyway, I'm sorry."

"You should be." He let out a big hiss of exasperation and wiped his mouth with the back of his hand. "Now get this poor, tired sonofabitch to the receiving barn."

Then he stomped off, shaking his head so hard his toupee flapped in the back.

"Jesus," I said to Lew, who'd been walking Moon's Medicine in a tight circle. "You were a lot of help."

"He wasn't chewing me out. Besides, he gets that way."

"Has he ever with you?" I led the mare out, and we headed for the receiving barn.

"Hell, yes. He's like one of those little dust devils: blows in, then blows right out again. He'll be okay in the morning."

"If you say so," I said as we slipped into line with the other horses for the fourth race. "I guess I should have known better."

"Yep."

"Do you know those guys, Fletcher and Grif?"

"Couple of crooks. The tall one's got a trainer's license."

"Is he any good?"

"He's got this routine where he talks owners into taking their horses away from one trainer and giving them to him. And he likes to grab 'em right when they're ready to run."

"So he gets the credit."

"Exactly."

"But why do people listen to him?"

"He's slick. You bit, didn't you?"

I blushed a little, but it was dark and I hoped Lew couldn't see. "Yeah, I guess I did."

"What happens here?" I asked as we led Moon's Medicine into the right stall in the receiving barn.

"The guy who identifies the horses comes around and

49

makes sure this is really who the program says it is. Then the track vet'll decide if the Moon will fall asleep in the starting gate or not."

The receiving barn was shadowy and quiet, with sparrows chirping softly in the rafters. Light from outside came through the narrow windows that ran just under the eaves and fell in long bars across the neatly raked soil, across the animals, across Lew and me.

"Here's your girlfriend," Lew whispered, pointing to Cara Mae, who was showing her stable pass at the door. "She wore those new white pants for you, pardner."

"Bullshit."

"You'll probably have to help her get those off tonight."

"I'm sure, Lew."

Cara Mae cut between a couple of horses and headed for the stall beside ours. When anybody nodded at her or said hi, she whipped her gun hand out of her pocket, made one finger into a barrel, and let him have it.

"Hi," I said as she passed, but she didn't even look my way.

"*Hola, que tal?*" she said real chummy to the guys handling the horse right next to ours, and I got this totally irrational pang of jealousy.

"She likes you," said Lew. "Don't worry."

"What are you, blind? She didn't even pretend to shoot me."

"You're a virgin, right?"

"At least keep your voice down. What if I am?"

"Have you ever felt a girl up?"

"Sort of. While we were dancing and stuff."

Lew smirked. "So who knows more about women —

you, who felt somebody up with your knees while you were dancing, or me?"

"All right, Mr. Sex, you do. So?"

"So she likes you. She wore those pants for you. She wouldn't bother to snub you if she didn't like you."

" 'Bye, Cara," I said as she passed us again on her way out.

Nothing. Not a blink.

"That was colder than last time," I said to Lew. "So according to your theory, she doesn't just like me. She loves me and wants to have my baby."

Jack was waiting for us in the saddling paddock.

"Watch what goes on here," Lew advised, "in case you have to do it by yourself some night."

Jack nodded, and we led the Moon in a wide circle, plodding behind a few of the other horses. The rest stood patiently in the open stalls. One or two whinnied and rolled their eyes.

Racing fans stood four deep, watching the trainers and handlers and horses, especially the horses. Everybody had a pencil and two or three newspapers. It looked like a convention of mad scientists scribbling at the equation that would change the world.

Jack drew a circle in the air with his forefinger, so we made yet another slow tour.

"What are all those people looking at?" I whispered to Lew.

"They think they're going to spot something: a bad leg, a bad attitude, who knows."

They talked, whispered, pointed, even laughed out

loud. I leaned into the Moon protectively. I felt like I'd taken my big, gangly kid sister down to the mall and right past the arcade.

Then Lew and Jack went to work, and I memorized the steps: sponge pad, saddle cloth, pommel pad, saddle. I patted the Moon one last time and she put her nose into my palm and shoved playfully.

"Come here," Jack said as the crowd melted away. And he slipped something into my palm. "Bet that for me."

"What is it?"

"Twenty bucks. To win."

"I thought you weren't going to bet tonight."

"The horse likes you. For all I know she likes running, too."

He took the bridle and Moon's Medicine followed him eagerly into the walking ring where owners gathered to shake hands with riders, listen to the pre-race strategies, and take one last look at their horses.

"What are they telling them?" I asked as all ten trainers got serious with all ten jockeys.

"To go to the front," said Lew, "and improve their position."

Then, looking like sets of fathers and sons, they walked across the grass to the waiting thoroughbreds, where the rider cocked one leg and the trainer helped him on.

"I'd like to do that," I told Lew as the horses filed out toward the track.

"Do what?"

"Give the jockey a boost."

"It's called putting the rider up," he said scornfully, "not giving the shrimp a boost. And only trainers do that, not certified shit-shovelers like you and me."

"I'd still like to do it," I said, almost to myself.

As Lew and I strolled through the air-conditioned grandstand, I remembered the money Jack had given me.

"I don't even know how to bet," I said, clutching the twenty.

"See those lines?" He pointed. "You just get in one, tell the clerk, 'Twenty to win on number six,' and that's it."

"And he remembers?"

Lew shook his head. "He punches a machine that spits out a ticket."

"I'd better get in line."

"Relax. Let's find the girls."

"What girls?"

Outside again, this time in front of the stands, the horses were filing by with their outriders.

"Lew! Over here!"

It was Abby in a white silk shirt with the top button undone. Both she and Lew had changed earrings. Hers had long feathers and his a little skeleton.

"Hi, Billy," she said as she put her arms around Lew. "Guess who's here." She nodded over his shoulder toward Cara Mae. "Why don't you mosey on over there."

"Yeah," said Lew. "And make sure you mosey. No strolling."

"What'll I say to her?"

"Anything," Lew advised. "Tell her you love those white pants."

"Don't say that," Abby broke in. "Just compliment her on her hat or something."

Some Stetson, great headgear, spiffy chapeau. I tried them all as I moseyed. Then I paused a few yards away. She was inspecting each and every horse. Intensely.

I inched closer. *Where'd you buy that hat? I'd like a hat like that. Can I try on your hat?*

"What the hell do you want?" she snapped.

The last thing I'd thought popped right out. "To try on your hat."

"Get bent," she said.

I reported to Abby and Lew.

"What'd you say?" Abby asked.

"That I wanted to try on her hat."

Silence.

"It just slipped out, okay?"

"So what'd she say?" asked Lew.

"She told me to get bent."

"Definitely promising," Lew said. "Definitely interested."

"Go back and try again," said Abby, shoving me.

"I have to bet."

"Yeah, let's bet. What'd your old man say, Abby?"

"That there's nothin' in here but the three horse."

I looked at the program. Number three was named Ted E. Bear.

"My uncle's got a friend named Ted he talks to on the phone."

"That settles it," Abby said. "Bet him with both hands."

"But he's the favorite," Lew complained, looking at the big electronic board across the track. "Even money."

"Everybody's using him in the Big Six," Abby declared.

"How does this odds thing work?" I asked.

Abby stared at me. "Lew said you weren't from here, but he didn't say you were from Mars."

"Look," said Lew patiently. "All those black numbers on the board that never change are the horses' numbers, okay?" He showed me the program. "Same as right here. And the neon ones underneath that change all the time are the odds."

"So the number one under the black three means if you bet a dollar you get a dollar back?"

"Now you're a gambler," he said. "Every neon number shows what you get if you bet a dollar: eight-to-one, six-to-one, whatever. But you can't bet a dollar. Minimum bet's two, which means at eight-to-one you get sixteen."

"That's all there is to it?"

"That's all."

I checked the Moon's number. "She's sixteen-to-one, and Jack wants me to bet twenty dollars." I was amazed. "Isn't that over three hundred bucks?"

"If he wins. Which he won't."

I looked for Cara Mae, but she was gone.

"Are you going to bet?" I asked.

"Maybe just the Big Six."

"What's that?"

"This gimmick where you have to pick six winners in a row. But it pays a fortune. C'mon, let's get in line."

Lew held the big door for me and we walked into the hubbub. He pointed. "You're there," he said. "There's a special window for the Big Six. I'll see you outside."

I hurried to the line he'd pointed out. I was clutching Jack's money so hard it'd gotten damp, and I was chanting, "Twenty to win, number six. Twenty to win, number six," when Cara stepped into the line beside mine.

"That horse hasn't got a chance," she said scornfully.

"That's what Lew says. Who are you voting for?"

"It's bet, not vote."

"That's what I meant." My line was moving faster than hers, so I turned around. "Who?"

"I'm not gonna yell it out," she hissed.

"Let's go, buddy," the guy behind me said right into my face.

When I turned around, I was at the window.

"Hello," I said to the clerk.

"What'll it be?" He looked as sleepy as Moon's Medicine.

"Uh, sixty to win twenty times."

"What is that in English?"

Oh, man. "What'd I say?"

"You said, 'Sixty to win twenty times.' "

"Let's go," shouted somebody behind me.

"I want to bet on the six horse." I pointed to the program. "To win."

"How much?" asked the clerk.

"Hey, let's go up there!"

"Here," and I pushed the wadded bill toward him.

He opened it up like I'd just blown my nose in it. "Twenty to win, number six," he said. "Right?"

"Thanks. Thanks a lot. Really." And I bolted.

"Wait!"

I turned around to see the ticket thrust out the window at me.

"Don't tell me drugs don't do things to their brains," said a woman as I grabbed the ticket and hurried away.

"Did you get down?"

"Huh?" I looked up to see Cara Mae shaking her head at the spectacle I'd made of myself. "You mean bet? Yeah, finally."

"I could see you were in trouble, but I was way back here." She shrugged helplessly.

"That's okay. Uh, look, about before. I didn't want to try on your hat. That was a mistake. I meant something else."

"You wanted to try on something else?" She took a step back.

"No, no. I meant I wanted to say something else."

"Like what?" She had her head cocked suspiciously.

"Well, anything but that."

Then she smiled for the first time. "C'mon," she said. "I'm afraid to leave you here by yourself."

We walked outside together and stood down by the rail. A long way off I could see the horses bunch behind the starting gate.

"Now can you tell me who you bet on?"

"You know those guys I talked to in the receiving barn?

They like their horse a little, so I bet him. But I used Ted E. Bear on my Big Six ticket."

"Seems like everybody bets that."

"You didn't? Hell, it could change your life just like that." She snapped her fingers.

I smiled politely.

"Well, maybe you don't need your life changed, buddy, but I sure as hell do."

Before I could say anything — I was just going to apologize again, since it seemed like everything I did made Cara mad — the announcer said, "They're off!"

Watching a horse race in person was nothing like watching it on TV. From where we stood, all the jockeys' silks melted together and the announcer's voice got lost in the crowd noise.

Cara Mae seemed to know what was going on, though, leaning forward, fists clenched, rocking a little, helping her horse on. "C'mon," she muttered. "C'mon."

Maybe because it wasn't my money I was more interested in her than in the race. Maybe I would've been, anyway, because there was something about her that got me excited. Her blond hair was parted on the side and cut short so some of it was always falling across one eye. Her legs looked great in those white jeans and she had smooth, brown arms with the fine hair bleached out golden. Her T-shirt had the word Ruffian printed across it, and she'd cut the bottom kind of jagged so that every now and then I could see the skin just above her belt.

"The favorite," she said with a shrug as the horses swept past us.

"Look, there's Moon's Medicine," I shouted.

"Damn," said Lew, who'd wandered over our way. "She got up for third."

"Does that help Jack?"

Lew shook his head. "They pay to show," he said, "but not when you bet to win."

"I won!" shouted Abby. "Thanks, Billy." She leaned forward and planted a big, wet kiss on my cheek.

"What'd I do?"

"Told me about that Ted guy your uncle knows. I love hunches. Plus I'm alive in the Big Six."

"Yeah," said Cara. "Me too."

"Then let's us have some beers and hang around. This could be our lucky night."

As things turned out it wasn't anybody's lucky night, but it was still fun. Between races we'd go to the saddling paddock and check out the horses, or at least Cara Mae would. Abby just bet whoever her father liked, and Lew admitted that he knew more about saddling a horse and giving it a bath than betting on it.

Cara wrote on her program, keeping it close to her chest like a poker hand. "Look at the gelding drop his hip," she said, and when I looked closely he did have a little limp. "And when they bob their heads like that? It means they're hurting on the opposite side."

I was pretty impressed, but I was just as impressed by being with her. She looked terrific; even her boots — run over at the heels and all scuffed up — were perfect. I was glad to stand beside her and have other people think she was with me, especially at the paddock, where I could sneak onto the step above hers and look taller.

"There goes that Big Six," moaned Abby when the winner of the seventh race was a horse that none of us had even considered.

"I'm dead, too." Cara Mae shook her head.

"C'mon," said Abby, "let's get out of here."

Cara said she had to go. "I'm riding home with Bev, I think."

"We'll take you," said Abby.

"Nah, that's okay."

Abby elbowed me, hard.

"C'mon with us," I gasped.

"We're out of here," said Lew, finishing his beer and destroying the cup with his combat boots.

"Everybody in the front," he said.

"Are you in the army?" Cara asked, looking at the truck.

"He *is* an army," Abby bragged. "Climb in."

There wasn't much room and I barely had time to cram my silly hat behind the seat before Cara ended up half on my lap.

"Something's poking me in the butt," she complained.

"That just means he likes you," said Abby.

"It's my scout knife," I explained as my face got hot.

"It's yours, honey. Call it whatever you want."

"Honest," I whispered to Cara, secretly vowing to stop carrying that stupid thing.

"Let's get some more beer," said Lew, angling across the dirt road that ran alongside the track. "C'mon, kid."

Inside, he grabbed a couple of six-packs. "I won a few bucks," he said. "This is on me."

Outside, Cara Mae and Abby were talking. I could see them through the huge window.

"What are they talking about?" I wondered.

"You and me. Just like we're talking about them."

"But we're not talking about them."

"We are now," he said. "Did you get good grades in English?"

"That's your idea of talking about girls?"

"Did you?"

"Pretty good. Why?"

"I'm out of things to tell Abby. You know how she likes to hear me talk about the bitter end. Can you remember anything I can use?"

"Gee, let me think a second." Here I was in line with another underage guy to buy some beer I didn't want, and all of a sudden I had to think back to sophomore English.

"There's always *carpe diem*," I said.

"What's that mean?"

"Seize the day."

"Like, don't wait, do it now?"

"Uh-huh."

He repeated it to himself. "Anything else?"

"How about 'The grave's a fine and private place,/But none, I think, do there embrace.' "

"Yeah, anything with a grave in it. Where's that from?"

"An old poem named 'To His Coy Mistress,' about a guy who asks his girlfriend to stop playing hard to get."

Lew rehearsed the lines until it was our turn.

"That's it?" asked the clerk, a young guy with a tragic complexion.

"Yeah, except for this little bit of advice. 'The grave's a fine and private place. But none, I think, do there embrace.'" Lew grinned down at me.

"Right. Let's see some ID."

I thought we'd had it, but Lew whipped out his wallet.

"Go on out toward Silverbell," said Cara as we settled in again. "Then take Shadow Road."

As we drove, Abby whispered in Lew's ear and they both laughed. Cara Mae looked out the window and I studied the long curve of her neck and her gold earring in the shape of a stirrup. Did everybody in the world have an earring but me?

"Are you okay?" I asked softly.

She shifted her arm, leaning into me a little more but still ready to spring away. She was wary as a wildcat.

"I was just thinking I should have used different horses in the Big Six, that's all."

"Next time."

"Sure," she said, not meaning it at all. Then she sat up and pointed past Lew. "Don't go up the lane. You'll wake my dad. I'll just walk from here."

"What about all this beer?" said Abby.

"Yeah," added Lew. "What about our little party?"

"I got horses in the morning."

"Just one beer," he said. "We'll park right up there."

Lew shifted gears, bounced across a drainage ditch, and shot up a good-sized hill, dodging rocks and cactus.

Cara and I held on and tried to keep from getting knocked out, while Abby hollered like a cowgirl.

"All right!" Lew said as we skidded to a stop.

Below us were the lights of Tucson. They were beautiful. They looked like loose diamonds scattered all over some jeweler's velvet cloth.

Almost immediately Abby and Lew started kissing like there was no tomorrow.

"Let's get out and stretch our legs," I said to Cara.

"Take some beer." Abby shoved a six-pack our way without looking.

When we closed the door, the little light on the ceiling went off. Moon or no moon, it was darker than I'd ever seen it. "Can you see?" Cara asked.

"Just barely. Hold on to my belt."

I pawed my way along the truck, quietly let down the tailgate, and we hopped on. My feet dangled in the air, and I was glad hers did, too.

"Want one of these?" I tapped on a beer can.

"Do you?"

"I'm kind of thirsty, actually."

"Me too. A little, anyway. Want to split one?"

I opened it right up and offered to let Cara Mae go first.

"Go ahead," she said.

"No, you."

"No, that's okay."

We were pushing it back and forth like a checker.

"Okay," she said finally.

I admit I liked putting my lips where hers had been; it was warmer there than the rest of the rim.

"I really do have a scout knife," I said, digging it out of my pocket."

"I believe you." She squinted into the gloom. "It looks like a nice one."

"Yeah, but it's a kid's thing. I don't know why I still carry it. I sure haven't had to fight off many bears lately."

"Maybe you're still a kid."

"I'm sixteen," I insisted.

"Yeah? Me too."

"Your last name's Whitney, right? Mine's Kennedy."

"I heard Abby call you Billy. Hi."

We shook hands in the dark like a couple of coal miners.

"Well," said Lew from the front, "if you don't want to seize the day, seize this," and Abby laughed one of her big outdoorsy laughs. Cara squirmed nervously.

"Abby seems pretty nice," I said, just to have something to say.

"Yeah. Well, she can afford to be. She's got all the money in the world, a mom and dad, and big boobs."

Then we just sat there again. I wasn't too anxious to try another pitiful line and get my head bit off. Then something moved in the darkness."

"What was that?"

"Coyote," she said.

"Are you sure?"

"Well, it's either that or a seven-foot monster with one eye."

I could see her white teeth: the second smile of the night.

"Why were you mad at me before?" I asked.

"I wasn't mad. It's not Abby's fault she's got every-thing."

"No, before that. Back at the track."

"Oh, that. Well, you know the old saying, 'Any friend of so-and-so's a friend of mine'? Well, I have a real hard time warming up to friends of Jack Ferguson."

"Lew told me what happened with that horse."

"Did he tell you maybe I had a good reason?" She hopped off the tailgate and took two or three quick steps.

"Look," I said, following her, "Jack's not always easy to get along with. He chewed me out good a little while ago."

"Why don't you just quit?" She whirled around. "I know all the trainers. I can get you on anywhere."

"I'm not so sure that's a good idea. I only got the job in the first place because my uncle knows Jack. Anyway, it's just for the summer."

"I knew you weren't from around here."

"Are you?"

"Don't I wish. But right after Labor Day I go to Phoe-nix, and Phoenix is the worst."

"Why's that?"

"Oh, I don't know. All those girls with their Lands' End sweaters and their perfect little haircuts."

"You can't stay here?"

"My dad's a racetracker. When the horses move, we move."

"My dad's a schoolteacher."

"God, I hate school. That's why I like Sundown Park, I guess. It's summer and I don't have to do anything but ride horses."

"Is that what you want to be, a jockey?" I was getting used to the dark and I could see her shake her head vigorously.

"Exercise girl. The minute I'm eighteen I'm getting on a bus and going right to Santa Anita racetrack and Charlie Whittingham, and I'm going to say, 'You're looking at the best exercise girl in the world and if you don't hire me you're crazy.' "

"Is he the best?"

She nodded. "And the track is and the people are and the horses are. He gets these million-dollar stallions from Europe and all over. Man, I'd love to sit on a million dollars and tell it to go fast."

" 'But none, I think,' " said Lew hoarsely, " 'do there embrace . . .' " And Abby moaned.

"Want to leave them alone for a few minutes?" I asked.

"Okay, but not too far in those tennies of yours. Last thing you want to do is step on a gila monster."

"What's a gila monster?"

"Big old beaded lizard, looks like a purse with teeth. He clamps on, it takes two paramedics to get him off."

"Actually, I'm fine here," I said, patting the tailgate.

"Oh, Lew," Abby crooned.

"C'mon," said Cara Mae, holding out her hand. "They're all asleep in their dens."

I followed her warily. Once I slipped off a little rock and she jerked me back on my feet before I could fall.

"You're really strong!" I said, and immediately wanted to bite my tongue. That wasn't the kind of thing you said to a girl.

"You try telling fifteen hundred pounds of horse what to do every morning, you'd be strong, too."

Then we stopped and just looked. The moon was low in the sky and one of the big old saguaros was outlined in front of it. A few cars felt their way along the road below us. Otherwise it was completely still.

"It's nice out here, isn't it."

"Yeah," she said, moving her hand restlessly in mine but not taking it away.

"My uncle's crazy about the desert. When I first got here, I thought he was nuts. Now I'm not so sure."

"It's nice, all right. I come up here sometimes by myself, just to try and think things out."

"Where's your house from here?" I asked.

"Couple hundred yards, but there's nothin' to see." Her voice had an edge to it again and I knew "nothin' to see" meant "don't go look."

Just then Lew honked the horn twice.

"I gotta go, anyway," she said.

"I'll walk you."

"I better walk you, at least back to the truck. I'll be fine. I know my way around here."

I was sorry to let go of her hand, but she needed it to smooth her hat brim and tuck in her T-shirt.

"See you guys." She tapped on the hood, and Lew and Abby waved through the window.

"See you tomorrow?" I asked, looking for her eyes under the hat.

"Sure." She turned and walked away. As I was about to open the door, though, she came back.

"You really need some boots," she said.

"Okay, I'll get some."

"And one more thing. Thanks for not bein' a jerk."

I looked down at my silly high-tops. She didn't know I'd wanted to kiss her. It's not that I was too much of a gentleman. I was too much of a coward.

"You're welcome," I said helplessly, but when I looked up she was already gone.

4

"I need some boots!" I said the minute my uncle walked in the door the next evening.

"Sounds like a major footwear emergency." He took off his black linen sport coat and hung it in the closet. Wes had been to see another trader. I knew he'd been in a plane and a car and probably at a reservation or two, and he still looked like he'd been kept on ice all day.

"How was Phoenix?"

"Hot. And I bought ten thousand bucks' worth of turquoise I hope I can sell. What's her name, by the way."

"Whose name?"

"The girl you want those boots for."

"It's not for a girl. It's so I won't get bit by a gila monster."

"Why does thinking about gila monsters make you blush?"

"Cara Mae Whitney," I said, looking at my socks.

"What size shoes do you wear?"

"Nine, why?"

"Follow me." He headed for his bedroom.

"I'll have to borrow the money and then pay you back. I get my first check from Jack in a couple of days."

"Not necessary." And he slid open one of the tall mirrored doors.

"Wow." Like a lot of things about Wes, his clothes closet looked like something out of *People* magazine. Dozens of shoes and boots pointed their toes at me. Every suit hung the same way, like a bunch of skinny guys standing in line. Everything was pressed and polished.

"If you really want her to think you're cool, try these black Tony Lamas."

"But they're yours."

"Billy, there're boots in there I've never worn. Like those. Go ahead."

"How come you've got so many?" I asked, grabbing, then sitting down to tug them on.

"I used to be a pathological shopper." He shook his head. "If I felt bad I'd buy something. If I felt awful, I'd buy two of them."

Slipping my cuffs down over the shiny tops, I stood up. For a second.

"Whoops," Wes said, holding out a hand for me to grab. "You'll get used to them. Maybe you ought to practice around the house, though. Your girlfriend's supposed to fall into your arms, not the other way around."

"She's not my girlfriend."

"Uh-huh," he said, like I'd just told him a cactus talked to me.

I sat down on the floor again and wrestled the boots off. I needed to practice walking, all right, but I'd do it later when nobody else was around.

"When did you stop being a maniac shopper? Or did you?"

"Well, mostly it didn't work. I was still scared to death. I was just well dressed and scared to death."

I stood up holding the new boots. "Scared of what?"

He looked me right in the eye, just like my dad did when he was serious. "Of getting AIDS. And of dying." But his voice wasn't low or gloomy. He was strangely matter-of-fact.

"You're not scared anymore?" I asked.

"Not like I used to be. Training for the AIDS hotline helped. I figure a couple of nights a week down there is better than prowling around the men's department at Goldwater's with a charge card in both hands." Then he glanced at his watch. "I need to take about three showers," he said, switching gears. "And a friend is coming by. Will you get the door?"

"Listen," I said, leaning in from the hall. "Thanks."

"Forget it. Enjoy!"

While Wes got cleaned up, I put my new boots back on and lurched from one piece of furniture to the next. I wondered if girls felt like this in their first high heels. I wondered if Cara Mae ever wore heels. It was hard for me to picture her in anything but boots. Or anywhere but on a horse or at least near one.

When the doorbell rang, I quickly wrestled the boots off again, carried them to the door, and threw it open.

"You must be Billy," said a giant. "I'm Luke Curtis." He grinned down at me. "Can I come in?"

"Oh, God. Sure."

It wasn't just that he was tall. It was his muscles, his ponytail, his earring, boots, tank top, wristband, and huge turquoise ring. When he moved, his leather pants creaked. He sounded like a saddle on the prowl. I tried to keep my eyes from bugging out.

"I'll, uh, tell Wes you're here."

"I'll tell him." Then he bellowed. "Wes, move your ass!" Next he strode to the bar and poured some club soda. "I like your boots, but wouldn't you say they're a little far from your feet?"

"I don't think I'm used to them yet. I keep falling over."

"About time," he boomed when Wes came out of the bedroom.

"How are you, Lucas?"

I looked at my uncle. There was something else in that question. Something like the stuff in one of my mom's recipes — a secret ingredient.

"I'm fine. Let's go." He glanced my way. "See you, kid. If Matthew, Mark, or John come by, tell 'em we went on ahead."

"Little biblical humor," Wes explained on his way out. Then he paused on the steps. "Will you be all right? There's some casserole left. Just put it in the microwave."

"I can take care of myself, honest."

"Well, then, at least put your boots on. The house could be crawling with gila monsters at any moment."

While the casserole nuked itself, I made a pretend-drink with Seven-Up, a lemon slice, and six olives. Then I tottered around the house. Wes had mirrors everywhere, so I could check out my progress whenever I wanted. Those boots sure made me look taller.

I had another Seven-Up — a double this time — and played this little game where I imagined what I'd give up to be big. Some hair: but did I want to be tall and bald? Some years: but did I want to be tall only until I was forty?

I wondered if Cara Mae would like my boots. I wondered if she'd like me more because I was taller. Suddenly I decided I'd call her up and say hi. She hadn't been at work, so I could just ask if she was okay. Chat her up. Maybe see if she wanted to go swimming tomorrow. In her bikini.

But there was no Whitney in the phone book, at least no Whitney on Shadow Road, and Directory Assistance was no help, either. I was amazed. I'd never known anybody who didn't have a phone.

Then, just like it knew I was thinking about it, the phone rang. I reached for a note pad: a lot of people called Wes.

"Billy? It's Dad. How are you?"

I loved hearing my dad's voice. It was strong and sure and just so real.

"I'm fine. I'm wearing my new cowboy boots." I picked one up just like he could see.

"Great. I used to wear those. Drove the girls crazy. I even had a Stetson."

"I need a hat, too." One of those tall ones like the guys at the track wore.

"So you're okay?" Dad asked.

"I like working on the backstretch," I said. "I like it more than I thought I would."

"Terrific. Listen, how's Wes?"

"Fine."

"He looks fine?"

"Uh-huh."

"He hasn't got a cold or anything that hangs on?"

"Dad, it's a hundred and three here every day."

"You're right. Sure. Are you two getting along?"

"He's pretty cool."

"He is, isn't he. It makes me want to see him. God, it's been years."

"He says the same thing."

"Well, there's not going to be many family reunions in Arizona if I spend all the money on long-distance calls. Just say hi to your mom. She really misses you, but I'm glad you're gone because now I don't have to eat anchovies on my pizza."

"Very funny, Dad."

"Take care, kiddo."

I talked to my mom for a second, then, and she told me she loved me, which is not a bad thing to hear. Then I hung up and ate my dinner. I was feeling pretty good in my new Tony Lamas. I wondered if Wes would let me use the van for a whole day, and if I could talk Cara Mae into going swimming.

When I heard a car door slam, I turned off the TV and met Wes right as he came in.

"Can I ask you something?"

He closed the door most of the way. "Turn off those lights."

"Why, what's up? Who's out there?"

"Go home!" somebody shouted. "You fucking faggots!"

"I'll bet," he said, "it isn't the Welcome Wagon."

"Cocksuckers! You dirty cocksuckers!"

"Go back in the living room, Billy."

My stomach started to get that quivery feeling like it always did just before I had to fight some guy after school.

"No, I'll stay with you."

He closed the door and bolted it. "Then let's both go in the living room."

I heard the clink of what was probably a beer can on the sidewalk. Then somebody put his foot to the floor and patched out.

" 'Another opening, another show,' " Wes said.

"What the hell was that all about?"

"We made the mistake of holding a healing service outdoors in the park on Fourth Avenue."

"Why were you at a healing service?"

"I went with Luke, but it never hurts to listen."

"Luke? What's the matter with Luke?"

"He has AIDS."

"You're kidding. He looks like an ad for vitamins."

Wes smiled. "Doesn't he. He goes to his yoga class, his acupuncturist, his nutritionist, his counselor, and he takes his AZT. He's everybody's role model, because when Luke had pneumonia nobody was sicker than he was. And now look at him. So people say, 'If Luke can do it, I can do it.' "

"And tonight those guys in the car just saw all the gays and started picking on you?"

Wes nodded, adding, "But we're not all gay. There's always a few straights, men and women. *And* a lot of old people who come because they get called names, too."

"I hate that. If I've heard 'Hey, shrimp' once, I've heard it a hundred times. And it always makes me wish I was big enough to kick their butts."

"Maybe," he said, "we could find some bozo who'd yell 'Hey, faggot. Hey, shrimp' at the same time and we'd both kick his butt."

I looked at him in surprise. "Would you do that?"

"Not very spiritually advanced, I admit, but an attractive fantasy."

It was sure fun picturing me punching some bigmouth out while Wes kicked him in the slats a few times with his two-hundred-dollar San Remo loafers.

Wes sat down heavily. "Can you find the whiskey?"

"I think so." I got up and went to the bar.

"Pour me about a quart, please."

"How about a little instead. That's what Dad does when he's upset." I tilted the bottle with the wild turkey on it. "Oh, he called tonight."

"Who did?" Wes asked absently.

"Dad. I told him you were fine, but that was before the vigilantes."

"They were just stupid kids," he said, swallowing about half the whiskey in one gulp. "Let's talk about some nice kids. Tell me about this girl you're breaking in those boots for."

"Cara? She *is* nice. Different from anybody I ever knew before. Kind of tough, on the outside, anyway. I don't have her figured all the way out yet."

"Well, let me give you some condoms."

"Pardon me?"

"Condoms. Rubbers. What do they call them in the Midwest?"

"We call them condoms or rubbers, but how'd we get from boots to . . ."

"You're old enough to be careful."

"I wouldn't get anybody pregnant."

"I'm not talking about that. I mean you're old enough to know that sex without some kind of protection puts you at risk."

"Cara hasn't got anything."

"It's unlikely, but she isn't the only girl you're ever going to sleep with."

"Who's sleeping? We've barely held *hands*. Wait, forget I said that. Now you'll probably want to give me a mitten."

He gulped the rest of his drink. "C'mon with me."

"Wes, I'm only sixteen."

"Kiddo, it's a whole new ballgame."

I followed him into the bedroom, where he reached into a drawer for some condoms. "Do you know how to use these?"

I took one of the foil packets and pretended to read. "Mix with vinegar and oil, shake, and pour on salad."

"These are not full of secret herbs and spices, smart ass."

"Look, if I take them, will you let me use the van tomorrow?"

"Is this condom blackmail?"

"I'll be careful," I said, looking at the handful of rubbers. "With everything."

5

Next morning I called Lew and told him not to pick me up.

"I've got my own wheels."

"Really? Then you could do me a favor. What if I went in right now and worked until ten or so, then you show up. That way one of us would be there all morning."

"Sure, I guess so."

"Edgar and I want to go out in the desert. It's worth a hundred bucks if I get home first."

"Are you driving the jeep or the truck?"

"Get real. We're on foot, nothing but a canteen and a knife."

"Both of you?"

"Sure. Mom drops us off in the middle of nowhere, we separate and race back."

"Boy, when my mom drops me off at the library I feel deprived if I have to walk home."

"How far is it?"

"At least ten blocks."

"My old man says we're all going to be in trouble after the firestorms, when there's looters and cannibals all over the place. Maybe you should go jogging this morning, start to prepare yourself."

"I think I'll buy a hat instead. I've got other things to prepare myself for."

"Does this mean you're getting rid of that straw thing your mom bought you? Definitely uncool. Pair of white shoes, a white belt, and that hat, you're in retirement, man. Sun City. Know what I mean?"

"Mom just didn't want me to get sunburned."

"Better dead than a weird head."

"Shakespeare, right?"

Lew snorted instead of laughing out loud. "Thanks for splitting the shift with me like this," he said. "If you run into any trouble, don't bother Jack. We'll work it out tomorrow.

"This won't take long, will it?" I asked Wes as I eased into a parking space at the mall. "I should be at the track in an hour or so."

"We only have to go to one store. If it's not in Ralph's House of Hats, you don't want it."

The mall was empty and cool at nine A.M. A few senior citizens were doing some toned-down race walking, and here and there a mom was leading her toddler around.

Ralph's wasn't open, but Wes knocked on the window and the owner waved and held up a wait-a-minute finger.

"Is Ralph gay?" I asked.

"Yes, but that's not why we're here. My dentist isn't gay, my accountant isn't gay, and I'd never go to a doctor who graduated last in his class just because he happened to look cute in a stethoscope."

"So Ralph just has good hats."

"Exactly."

Inside, I looked around as Ralph and Wes talked. "You heard about Michael?" Wes said. Then I wandered out of range.

There were a thousand hats, but not that many Western ones. I took a couple off their pegs and found a three-way mirror. The first one — gray with a lizard band — fit me exactly like a thimble fits the end of a pencil. With it on, I couldn't see a thing. I whipped it off and slammed on a white one. It must have been made for a Munchkin; it just perched up on my head. After that I didn't even take them to the mirror. I'd just slide them off the peg, onto my head, and right off again.

"Any luck?" Wes asked as I wandered past.

"I don't know."

"Here." He plucked a black one off the wall beside him, and, before I could stop him, put it on me.

I walked to the nearest mirror.

"It's you," cried Ralph.

"No, it's not. It's a hat." I bit off the last word like my mom did when she was cranky.

"Maybe," Wes said to his friend, "I should confer with the customer in private." We watched Ralph retreat, then Wes asked me what was wrong. "It looks great on you, kid."

"I look like Black Bart. Besides, it costs too much." I showed him the price tag. "Sixty dollars."

"Forget the money."

"But I want to pay for something myself. You already gave me the boots."

"So I'll give you a hat, too."

"No, Wes."

"Why not? I want to."

"I'm working now. I've got my own money. I can pick it out myself and pay for it myself. I don't need a committee." I looked down at my boots, then at him. "You know what I mean?"

"What kind of hat do you really want?"

"I think I saw it on the way into the mall."

"Ralph," he half shouted to his friend, "thanks a lot."

Two minutes later we were standing in front of a table just inside a store called Miller's Outpost. There must have been a hundred hats, all the same cream color, all with tall crowns and curved brims, all with feathers in the paisley bands. A big sign said $11.95.

I tried them on until I found one that fit. Then I turned to Wes. "Okay?" I asked.

"The black one was very distinctive," he said.

"But that's the point. I don't want to look distinctive. I want to look like the other guys."

Jack was hunched over his books when I knocked on the door to the office.

"Good," he said. "It's you. Lew just left."

"Is it okay if we split things up like this?"

"Long as the work gets done."

"I was out buying a hat." I posed in the doorway.

"Uh-huh," he said without looking up from his ledger.

I worked hard for a couple of hours cleaning stalls, mixing feed, and cooling out Oxley Girl and Captain Poetry after they'd both worked a mile. Every once in a while I'd slip into the bathroom and look at myself in the mirror, tilting my hat this way and that, trying to decide if I wanted to look cocky, sinister, or cool.

I had my eye out all the time, though, for Cara Mae. The van — for today, anyway, my van — was waiting in the parking lot. Inside the van, on the seat, was my swimsuit. Under the seat lurked those condoms.

I felt completely overprepared, like the guy who calls the weather bureau, finds out it'll be sunny and warm, then heads out wearing a raincoat anyway.

I barely knew Cara Mae. What if she dropped an earring, reached under the seat for it, and came up with a box of rubbers! I couldn't hear myself saying, "Oh, my uncle gave us those. His motto is Better Safe Than Sorry."

All of a sudden I stopped thinking about Cara, stopped hosing out the wheelbarrow, stopped everything. Something was up. It was too quiet. There wasn't any straw crackling; there weren't those random knocks and bumps. And that meant Moon's Medicine wasn't pacing around in her stall like a worried mother on prom night.

When I peeked around the corner, the Moon was staring out of her stall at a chicken. It was the first time I'd seen the mare stand still when she wasn't worn out.

Carefully I slipped up beside her. She nuzzled me, then gazed down at her new pal. I know chickens can't grin with those hard little mouths of theirs, but this one was getting close.

"What's going on here?" I said, half out loud.

I leaned down and picked up the chicken. The Moon's big head followed me. Total eye contact between those two. It was like that old song, "Some enchanted evening, you will meet a stranger." What could be stranger than this?

When I put the chicken on the little ledge, Moon's Medicine sniffed it all over, the gusts from her big nostrils ruffling the white feathers. Then the chicken sat down primly and looked around.

I slipped down to where we kept the feed, got a handful of corn, and spread it out where they could both get at it. They nibbled around until there were only a couple of kernels left. Then Moon's Medicine politely nosed them toward the hen, who daintily finished up, then looked into the mare's eyes. Deeply.

About half an hour later I saw Cara Mae on a stable pony. Her hat was pulled down and she was slumped in the saddle.

"Hi," I said, taking the bridle in my hand.

"Oh, hi."

"What's the matter?" I asked.

"I feel like I've been rode hard and put up hot."

I liked the sound of that but had no idea what it meant, so I just shrugged.

"I've got a little hangover," she explained.

"Is that why you didn't come in yesterday? I thought maybe you were sick."

She inspected me from behind her sunglasses. "What's different about you?" She asked dully.

"Start at my head."

"Hey, you got rid of that old guy's hat."

"Yeah."

"Not bad."

"Not as good as yours." I took my new hat off. It was stiff and hard. "It's too new."

"Get it wet."

"Really?"

"Uh-huh. Then wear it while it dries. Pretty soon it'll be like part of you."

"Notice anything else?"

She smiled just a little. "You're funny."

I pulled up one pants leg, hoping for another smile. "Anything about my feet?"

"Hey," she said, coming out of it even more. "Tony Lamas."

"Yeah. Now come on over to the barn. Just follow the wobbling boots."

I walked beside her for a dozen yards, my shoulder brushing against her thigh, grateful that the pony was there to lean on. I held out my hand then, but she slid out of the saddle on her own, right in front of the odd couple.

"What?"

I pointed into the stall, where Chicken Little was roosting happily in one corner. The mare stood over her protectively.

"Hey, you cured her!" Cara Mae exclaimed. "She's not walking around anymore. She'll win next time."

"Want to go swimming?"

"Huh?"

Was I smooth, or what? "I, uh, was wondering if you wanted to go swimming later, maybe. I mean after we both marvel at this for a while."

We looked in at the happy couple.

85

"What is this, a date?"

"Yeah, I guess. Is that okay?"

Neither of us was even looking at the other person. We were talking to the animals.

"I don't have my suit," she said, frowning.

I moved a little so my bare arm touched hers. "We could drive by your house. It's on the way to this water park I keep seeing ads for. Surf's Up."

"Oh, yeah!" She turned to me eagerly. "I always wanted to go there. Everybody's been but me."

"So what are we waiting for?"

"Wow!" Cara bounced on the seat, put her face up close to the air-conditioning vent, and ran the electric windows up and down a few times. "This is really cool. I should of taken my boots off and stuck 'em in the back."

"It's okay. Wes isn't that fussy about his stuff."

"Is he rich, your uncle?"

"I guess he is in a way. But he works and everything."

"You know, I could make twenty thousand a year easy working on the West Coast at Hollywood Park or Santa Anita." She sat back in the seat and repeated dreamily, "Twenty thousand bucks. I could buy anything I wanted with that."

As Cara Mae fantasized, I drove carefully toward Shadow Road. I'd never driven with a girl all by myself. I had wheels, a tankful of gas, spending money. I could go anywhere, and anything — absolutely anything — could happen.

"Is your uncle married?" asked Cara as I glided off the highway.

"Uh, no."

"Divorced or anything? Kids?"

"Wes isn't your average guy."

"Tell me about it. This isn't your average van."

"I mean he's not like you and me."

"What is he, Mexican?"

"Not different like nationality or anything." I was glad to turn down the road that led to her place. "Which driveway?" I asked.

"Look, I better just run up and get my stuff. Dad might be asleep."

Instead of thinking about what I'd got myself into, I watched her disappear around a curve. I admired the way she could run in her boots. Frankly, I still felt a lot better *standing* in my Tony Lamas.

Thinking about myself more or less nailed to the floor made me grin, but thinking about Wes and what Cara Mae might say wiped the grin away. What if it mattered to her that he was gay? What if, when I told her, she'd say "ugh," and wouldn't even sit by me?

And what if, said a little voice, *you stop thinking like a jerk. Wes is a terrific guy. You're driving his car, eating his food, and sleeping under his roof. So stop acting like you're ashamed of him.*

"He's gay," I blurted as she climbed back into the car.

She tossed her suit and towel into the back seat. "Who is?"

"My uncle."

She looked down at her scuffed-up boots, put the heels together, and sighted between the toes. "That's okay, I guess."

"Really?"

She shrugged. "Don't you have kids like that where you come from?"

"Sure."

"So no big deal."

"It's just . . . I mean back home I leave those guys alone. They go their way and I go mine. But living with Wes is different."

"Guys have called me queer," she admitted.

"You're kidding."

"When I wouldn't go out with 'em or if I did when I wouldn't do stuff. They'd say I never wore a dress, then they'd call me a dyke."

"People are really stupid sometimes, aren't they?"

Cara Mae slouched in the seat and pressed her hat down with both hands like we were in a high wind. "Why am I telling you all this stuff, anyway." She plunged one hand into her purse and came up with a Bic and some Camel filters. "I thought," she said through a smoke screen, "we were going swimming."

Right out in the middle of the desert somebody had built a miniature California: sand, surf, volleyball, blond-haired kids in baggy trunks, Coppertone, sunblock, white zinc noses, bikinis, the works. Plus long twisty water slides for thrills and inner-tube lagoons to just splash around in.

Cara Mae was like a little kid, sitting right up close to the window, jiggling one leg, pointing out primo parking places, being really wiggly in line. When I put my arm around her shoulders as we waited, I could feel her breathing, she was that excited.

"See you in a minute," she said, dashing into the dressing room. Cara Mae could really make me smile. I guess it was true that she could be moody, but when she was up the energy just shot off her.

I didn't feel so perky, though, when I started to take my clothes off and put stuff in the locker. There is just no way to look tall in the nude; no cowboy-type zoris with big heels, for instance. There I was in all my shortness. And my paleness. So I looked around and started comparing. If that isn't the worst. Somebody's always bigger, longer, stronger, or more tanned. And to find somebody I could outdo, I had to pick on kids about thirteen who were still growing or so pale they'd probably just got out of the hospital.

Still, nobody stared at me, not really, while I waited for Cara Mae. I wasn't the only kid wearing his trunks and his cowboy hat. And I forgot about myself, anyway, when the girls started to walk by in little bunches of two and three like they do. Some of them were spectacular in those suits that must have come from L.A.: big holes in interesting places, straps and rings and strings that they kept having to adjust like parts of some strange musical instrument. Then my all-time favorite strolled by — a redhead in just a few scraps of purple cloth, the bottom one about as big as a bruise. Who designed those things? Maybe I could get into the swimsuit business?

"Think she's cute?" Cara asked, appearing beside me.

"Yeah," I said, blushing at getting caught.

She beaned me softly with her towel. "I was pretty sure you weren't thinking about throwing a blanket over her."

We did everything there was to do — slid down the slides, got knocked over by the surf, and bobbed around on inner tubes. Cara's suit — which had Plutos all over it — was old and the elastic was stretched out, so she was always having to rearrange it, not like those beauty queens I mentioned with their fraction-of-an-inch read-justments, but real tugs just to keep things covered up. She'd pop out of the water laughing, then cuss and pull at her top or bottom or both.

It was funny in a way, but it also made me horny out of my mind. Once I saw just about her entire left boob and more than once — just because of the way she was floating on her back or sprawled in her yellow tube — this little hollow way up at the inside of her thigh. It was such a smooth and secret little place that I got that hot and woozy feeling, meaning I was rapidly approaching core meltdown.

My folks had been great about sex, talking to me about it when I was young, always being honest and out in the open about most stuff. I told my dad once in a roundabout way that I had these feelings and thoughts that I wouldn't want anybody to know about. He just said that everybody had those. "You and Mom?" I asked. And he said, "Yep."

"Billy, I'm tired," said Cara Mae crawling out of the surf toward me. There was that left boob again.

We found a couple of chaises off by themselves and lay down.

"Would you mind putting stuff on my back?" she asked.

Would I *mind*? I would've *paid* to. I said, "Sure, why not."

It was as nice as I expected. She was so strong and lean that she reminded me of an otter — wet and gleaming and sleek and taut. But I've never seen that in a poem. "My love is like a red, red rose" is fine, but "My love is like an otter"?

But she wasn't my love. She wasn't even my girlfriend. She was a girl who was a friend.

"Your turn," she said as I finished.

I rolled over and stared down at the concrete as she squirted the stuff on me in a long line like Cheez Whiz. She wasn't as smooth and as slow a massager as I was, but I was hoping to make the job last till Wednesday. All of a sudden I started to get one of those stupendous erections. And, if that wasn't bad enough, the lounges we were on had criss-crossed plastic webbing and my pecker was telescoping down at an angle into one of those spaces. If a gun went off and everybody jumped up, there I'd be with a chaise attached like a shield: Sir Hard-On.

I decided to try and get my mind off it. Cara and I were lying with our heads turned so we could see each other.

"Did you always know you wanted to ride horses?" I asked.

"Uh-huh. There's a picture of me in a little yellow dress with my legs straight out on top of an old Appy named Shining in the Wind. I don't think I'll ever forget what it felt like to look down and see the top of my momma's hat."

What a terrific picture! My mom had one of me like that, but I was on a mechanical horse in front of Thrifty's Pharmacy.

"You're lucky. I still don't know what to do exactly except go to college."

"Not me." Her head rocked gently and a drop of water slid from her forehead, past her nose, right to her lips. "College takes too long."

Talking about the future was a surefire erection chaser. Every kid I knew, including me, was dying to grow up. But then what? Just thinking about it was depressing.

"I'm thinking about not even finishing high school."

"Gee, what would you do?"

"Just ride all the time, maybe go on over to the Coast."

"Aw, you ought to finish. A high school diploma's something to be proud of."

"I know what you should be, Billy. You should be a high school counselor."

I grinned back. "I guess my folks really drilled it into me about finishing anything I started."

"I don't know. If I'm eating a bad meal, I don't want to just keep on and get even sicker." She rolled over and readjusted her suit. "Can I have the lotion? I don't want to burn the tops of my feet."

I watched her smooth Coppertone on her long legs. Quitting high school was a radical idea for me. In Bradleyville, the kids who did that were either pregnant, complete stoners, or both. Cara Mae was the first person I'd met who ever wanted to drop out so she could *do* something. And, of course, there was me, the future veterinarian-trainer-swimsuit designer.

We just lay there for a while. Then I slid my hand across and covered hers. She turned dreamily.

"Hi, cowboy," she said.

"Hi. How's your hangover?"

"Almost gone. I might sleep a little. If I snore, poke me."

I sat up and looked around, inspected my knees for signs of the dreaded sunburn, put on more lotion everywhere, tried to scope out the cutest girls. When a cloud drifted over the sun a few minutes later, Cara Mae sat up and shivered.

"Do you ever not look forward to waking up in the morning 'cause it's just even money you're gonna be depressed?"

If she'd given me a second to answer, I'd have said no. But she didn't.

"I just open my eyes and then wait a second or two to see who's in charge."

"My dad says being a teenager is hard. He says he wouldn't go back for anything."

"Did your mom run away?"

"God, no. She's . . ."

"Mine did."

"Really?"

"I didn't cry or anything. She just came up to my room real late one night about ten years ago. She was wearing this silvery shirt with black fringe that she only wore when she was barrel-racing, so I knew something was up." Cara squirmed a little and the chaise swayed. "She sat down on the edge of my bed — I remember we were in Prescott and it was raining — and she said

that she just had to get out of there or she was gonna
die. And I probably wouldn't understand until I was
grown."

"Do you?" I asked softly.

"Understand? Not yet. But more than I did, maybe,
two years ago even. See, now I don't want to stay put,
either."

It was nine o'clock. I turned off the ignition and the
enormous night came pouring into the front seat of the
van.

Cara said, "We got up here about five times faster than
in Lew's stupid old truck." Then she leaned toward the
elaborate dashboard. "Can I play a tape?"

"Sure." I looked out at the same distant lights and, in
the pitch dark, wiped my palms dry on my jeans. I didn't
want to hold her hand and have it feel like I was wearing
a wet glove.

"Man," she said as Paul Simon came out of the stereo
speakers, "if we had a refrigerator we could live in here.
Sleep in the back, drive all over the country seeing different racetracks."

Clumsily I put my hand on her shoulder.

"What?" She turned toward me.

"Nothing." I took my hand back, frowning at it like
it'd jumped up there on its own. "Uh, what was that
thing I ate at the Double L?"

"Chili relleno." She gave it a little Spanish twist. "Pretty
good, huh? And cheap. I love that restaurant."

I wanted to kiss her, but all I could do was make inane

conversation and pat her on the back. If I kept banging on her shoulder she'd get fed up or bruised or both.

She was so pretty. Usually there was a crease or two right between her eyebrows, like she was trying to figure something out, but the moonlight erased everything. Her face was so smooth, and I loved it when her tongue came out and licked her lips. Maybe I could just tell her to relax and let me do that.

"You look pretty in the moonlight," I said softly.

She sat up abruptly. "I look like a horse."

Everything had changed. She'd been in a good mood ever since dinner, but suddenly she wasn't anymore. It was like one of those cold snaps that comes on just like that and ruins the crops.

"You don't either."

"Look at me."

"I've been looking at you."

"Really look." She showed me her profile. "Here's the long, horsey face." She pulled at her hair. "Here's the mane. That's why people look at me funny, 'cause they can't tell if I'm a horse or a girl."

"Everybody thinks people are looking at them. I do."

"You? What for?"

"Because I'm short. I think people are saying to themselves, 'What a shrimp. He'd be okay if he was only a foot or so taller.' "

"How tall are you?"

"Five four and a quarter."

"That's plenty tall. People aren't talking about you being little."

"Yeah? Well, they aren't talking about you being a horse, either."

She fell back into the seat with a sigh. "You must think I'm a real nutcase."

"I just think you're pretty."

Cara Mae looked down at the floor, kicking at the plush carpet with her boot heel. "Want to smoke a little dope?" she said, beginning to rummage in her purse.

I shook my head. Maybe it was those films in Health Ed, but I had this weird fear of starting out with grass and ending up ten days later on heroin. Then I'd be the subject of an after-school special, "The Littlest Addict." No thanks.

"Okay if I do?"

I shrugged.

"Sometimes it feels like my head's a cheap hotel with everybody yellin' at everybody else and I'm the night clerk." She took a wrinkled-looking joint out of a tin box with a panther on the front, lit up, and inhaled. "This stuff," she wheezed, "kind of shuts everybody up."

Politely she rolled the window all the way down and exhaled into the dark, then offered me the last half-inch. I have to admit, she did seem calmer.

"Better not," I said. "I have to drive home."

"You know," she said softly, "you're the one who's cute."

"Oh, sure."

"I mean it. You got skin most girls would kill for."

It's a wonder I didn't glow in the dark like a stoplight.

"You're loaded."

"A little."

"Can I kiss you?" I asked suddenly.

"If you want to."

I leaned into her side of the car. Cara's lips were dry, but her mouth was open a little and I was faced with the age-old dilemma of whether to stick my tongue in there or not. So I did, and it was great.

"Wow," she said after about a minute. "You're sure not queer."

"Gay," I corrected automatically.

"Yeah, right." She leaned toward me, then drew back suspiciously. "You're not one of those guys who'll do it to anything, are you?"

"Anything but a gila monster."

Cara started to laugh. "You're really screwy," she said. "I like that."

I liked being with her, too. Some dates are just nerve-wracking. This one was easy, a lot easier than I expected. Even if I said something silly, it didn't seem to matter.

Cara leaned forward and turned up the volume on the cassette player. On came "Bridge Over Troubled Waters." "You think this means something?" she asked, getting serious.

"The song?"

"Everything. The song, the stars, those houses down there. Us."

"Gee, I don't know." I reached to touch her face, being careful so I wouldn't put an eye out. When she turned toward me, we kissed again. I wasn't sure what to do with my other hand, so I just let it settle on her side, right where I could feel her ribs. Immediately one of her hands came down to keep mine in place: a classic move.

I don't know why anthropologists are so busy with African or American Indian rituals. Local teenagers have them by the millions: little kiss, hand on side, hand number two to the rescue, hand number one inches toward the Sacred Bra, both hands engage in mini-struggle. If there'd only been beating drums and a torch or two, it'd go right in the *National Geographic*.

I didn't even mind. What was she supposed to do, just sit there and let me? And what if she had, then what? Did I suavely reach under the seat and whip out a prophylactic?

Cara Mae pushed herself away gently. "I gotta go," she said. "And you're not even breathing hard. Do you do this all the time?"

"I don't even stop for lunch."

She grinned at me. "I like being with you. You're not all serious like some guys."

"I like being with you, too." Then we kissed a little more.

"Really, Billy," she gasped, sitting up and reaching for her hat. "My dad'll be thinking the worst."

"He's not mean to you or anything, is he?" I asked, to keep her in the van a few minutes longer.

"My dad? Nah. He's just a clerk at the track."

"Really? Which one? What's he look like?"

"You'd never notice him. He's always like in the back row of the picture on the end. Know what I mean?"

"I guess so. I'll drive you home."

But she was out of the car again, just like last time. "No problem. See you tomorrow."

Then I was alone with an erection that could've etched Cara Mae Whitney on the windshield. Instead, I drove it home and about halfway there it got the idea, curled up, and went to sleep.

6

"Are you still putting flax seed in her feed?" demanded Jack, barging into the stall where Lew and I were working.

"You told us not to week before last."

"Then why does she look so good? I don't want her looking good. Now take a curry comb and rough her up some."

"Jack," Lew said, "she's wrapped on all four legs now. Who's going to want her?"

"Just do it, son," he shouted back at us.

Lew grinned at me. "He's wearing his Winner's Circle toupee."

"Are you going to bet?"

"Sure." He stepped around the Moon's chicken carefully, his big combat boot settling in the crisp straw. "You don't get many chances like this. We'll get ten-to-one or better."

"Why does Jack want her to look so bad? I'm proud of the way she's come around."

"All trainers are paranoid." He waved my question away, then looked up expectantly. "Before we were so rudely interrupted, you and Cara were parked up on the hill."

"Will you take off that hat first? I can't talk seriously to a guy wearing a hat that says We Are the Children of a Dying Generation. Where'd you get that, anyway?"

"Out at the punk shop on Broadway." He stuffed the cap — a baseball cap, no less — into his back pocket. "Now."

"Okay. We park up there just about every night Wes'll let me use the van."

"And?"

"And we fool around."

"You nail her, right?"

"No," I protested.

"But you feel her up?"

"Sort of."

"Do you get your hand in her pants?"

"Sometimes, but her jeans are so tight it gets numb and goes to sleep."

Lew stood up and started to brush Moon's Medicine, pushing against the smooth gray coat. "So when are you going to nail her?"

"Will you stop calling it that? It makes me feel like a carpenter."

"Well, what would you call it?"

"I don't know, maybe sleeping together, maybe . . ."

"Well, sure. Your hand's already asleep, so you've got a head start."

"Or making love."

"Fine, call it whatever you want, but when are you gonna do it?"

"I'm not sure she really wants to. I'm not even sure I want to."

I slipped the bridle on the mare. She leaned down to say goodbye to the hen, almost blowing her off her feet.

"Are you nuts? You're sixteen, you're away from home, and you've got this girl who likes you. This is the Magic Summer, Billy. You're never gonna be the same after this one. You'll know stuff, important stuff."

"Let's go," said Jack, appearing again, then setting off without us. His Winner's Circle toupee had a pompadour as big as a hood ornament. Real natural-looking. From about a mile away.

"Why does he wear that thing?" I ducked down a little and whispered to Lew under the mare's neck.

"Why do you wear those striped shirts? Think you look taller, right?"

I flushed like all my blood had lit up.

"You're tall enough and, anyway, we're all the same size lyin' down." He leered over the gray mane at me. "Know what I mean?"

"Can I ask you something?"

"Speaking of sex?"

"Sort of."

"About Cara?"

"Sort of."

"About life in general?"

"Sort of."

"Okay, let's have it."

"Did you ever wear cowboy boots?"

"This is the question about sex, Cara, and life?"

"Did you?"

"A long time ago."

"Did they hurt your feet?"

"At first."

"My feet are killing me."

"Wear your tennies."

"Not on your life."

"How is she?" Cara asked even before she kissed me hello.

"Great. She just wants to get back to her roommate."

Cara shushed me, glancing around at the bettors standing near us.

"Hot damn," Abby said. "I love this to death. Look at those odds."

Moon's Medicine was fourteen-to-one. That was almost thirty dollars for two. Almost three hundred for twenty.

"Let's get in line," said Lew. "If I got shut out I'd off myself."

"Look," Cara Mae whispered. "Everybody get in a different line."

"Why?" I asked.

"I don't want people to see all of us and put two and two together."

I looked around helplessly. I'd been betting a little the last couple of weeks, but the finer points still eluded me.

"Jack's wearing his Winner's Circle toupee," Lew said. "If that isn't a tipoff, what is?"

"Will you all just do it?" Cara pleaded.

"Sure," Abby said. "No reason to get the crowd all

hot and bothered. Let's just meet right back here soon as we're done, okay?"

I got in line knowing I had six dollars I could spare, but that was all I knew, except I didn't want to lose it. What if the Moon was thinking about her chicken and then ran like one? What if she took a bad step out of the gate and ended up behind eleven other horses? What if? What if?

When it was my turn, the clerk looked up expectantly.

"Six dollars," I said.

His fingers hovered over the numbered buttons in front of him. "To . . . ?"

"No, six."

"I know, I know. But six dollars to do what: win, place, or show?"

"Oh." What if. What if. "What do *you* think?"

"Are you sixteen?" he demanded. "You got to be sixteen to bet in this place."

"Place," I blurted. "Six dollars to place."

When the horses were loading into the gate, Cara Mae held my hand so tight I thought she was going to break something. Even Abby was tense, doing a nervous little dance on the cluttered bricks. Lew patted me on the shoulder.

"Won't be long now," he said, rubbing his lucky earring.

We were all clutching our tickets like they were passports and we were about to escape from Russia.

"Oh, shit!" We said it together like a Greek chorus.

Moon's Medicine had been bumped hard coming out of the gate. The jockey — a kid named Pedroza not much older than I was — got right into her, though, and she was moving through the pack.

Cara let go of my hand and, like she always did, started to drift toward the rail. She had her jaw set and she was banging her clenched fists on her thighs. The crowd was starting in behind us. Abby and Lew were yelling. I was yelling, too, because I could see the Moon loom behind the three front-runners lined across the track. I could see Pedroza switch the whip and get into her left-handed. Moon's Medicine dug in, angling outside the early speed as they flashed by. She was gaining at every step when the wire came up.

The noise died behind us. "She got it, didn't she?" Cara insisted. "She got up."

We all looked at the glowing sign — PHOTO.

"Hard to tell," said Lew doubtfully.

"Nah, she got it easy. You saw it, Billy."

"I couldn't tell."

"Abby?"

"I don't know, sugar. Maybe."

"Oh, man. You guys are a real drag."

One of the things I liked about Cara was that she was passionate. I don't mean in that way, necessarily. I mean she had big feelings. When she said that the rest of us were a drag she didn't really mean it. She was just having a big feeling.

I knew enough to just leave her alone. She did this thing I'd seen before when we were waiting for a photo finish, turning around and facing the stands, eyes shut, chanting the number she wanted: "Seven, seven, seven, seven."

When the crowd roared, she whirled around.

"Oh, no." She stamped her foot. "Oh, no. Sonofa-bitch." Cara stared at the crumpled ticket in her hand, then tore it to shreds, threw it down, and spit on it. "I'm going home!" she announced.

"C'mon, don't," I said.

"I just lost forty-four dollars. What am I supposed to do, go out and have fun?"

"We all lost," Abby reminded her. "That was forty I'd saved."

"Take it easy," cautioned Lew. "We all lost."

I looked at the number seven glowing on the board right under the winner's. "Actually," I said, "I bet to place."

"You did what?" Cara Mae demanded.

"Good for you," said Abby.

"I was all mixed up. It was just an accident that I won."

"You get eighteen bucks back," Lew said as the prices came up. "You buy the beer."

"Why didn't you tell me you were gonna bet to place," said Cara Mae. "I might of, too."

"You're the one wanted us all in different lines," I reminded her. "Besides, you always bet to win, you told me so."

"Well, I might not have this time."

"How am I supposed to know that? And what am I

supposed to say? 'Hey, I'm confused. Why don't you get confused too?' "

"I'm going home," she said, turning away.

"Don't. C'mon let's . . ."

"Let her go," said Lew.

Abby put her hand on my shoulder. "Yeah, she'll cool down."

"Abby!" Mr. Dayton bellowed from the bar.

Lew cringed. "Doesn't your old man ever do anything but yell?"

"He's mad, too, just like Cara. He truly hates to lose."

"Abby!"

"Tell him to shove it," muttered Lew.

"I'll be right back." She turned and ran, holding her hat on with one hand.

"Maybe your uncle's got something," said Lew. "If we were queer, you and I could go out."

"Gay," I said out of habit.

"I should have known tonight wasn't my night." He crushed the empty beer cup he was holding. "Guess what I got in the mail today. My grades. I failed math. I'm not getting my diploma."

"Your school didn't have commencement yet?"

"Who goes to that stupid stuff. They just got their computer to send their grades out is all I know, and Sanchez gave me an F in math." He looked over his shoulder, turning enough for me to see the skull he'd sketched on the back of his T-shirt. Abby was arguing with her father now. His big hat — twice as big as mine, making it the twenty-gallon model — jiggled as he shook his finger at his daughter.

"Let's go," said Lew. "She's history tonight. Her old man'll be on her case for hours."

Horses can't just be shoved back into their stalls after they've run; they have to be cooled down slowly. Lew and I walked the mare around and around for thirty minutes, then gave her a bath and something special to eat, mash saturated with Guinness stout. She was real glad to see the chicken, who'd slept through the race. But the bird got up when she came in, and they had a touching reunion.

Lew and I were almost finished scraping the horse dry when I asked him, "Does Abby ever get depressed?"

"When she gets her period, she's a pain in the ass."

"Not that so much. I mean just depressed."

"Like when she wants to fly to Phoenix to shop and her dad won't let her?"

I shook my head. "Cara says she doesn't want to go out or eat or do anything sometimes because she's just so screwed up, but she doesn't know why. It just sort of drops down on her."

"Women are like that. It's supposed to keep you guessing. They think guys are like fish — give 'em a little line, reel 'em in, give 'em a little, reel 'em in."

"That doesn't sound like Cara." I patted Moon's Medicine one more time, stepped outside, and clicked the stall door shut behind us.

"Aren't you telling me," said Lew, not letting go of

the subject, "that you go almost all the way with her one night and then almost nowhere the next?"

"I'm just saying I don't think it's on purpose, that's all."

"Hey, I didn't say they knew what they were doing." He picked up a pair of electric clippers that we used for the horses, plugged them in, and, looking right at me like I was a mirror, ran them down the center of his crewcut, leaving a two-inch swath. "Is that cool?" he asked.

"I think *you'll* like it."

When Lew dropped me off at home a few minutes later, I knew something was wrong. Wes's van was parked at an angle in the drive. Nothing Wes did or touched was ever catty-cornered, not a knife and fork, not a hairbrush, not a magazine.

Carefully I opened the front door and peeked in. It was pitch dark. That was scary. We always left a light on for each other. I dropped on my belly and slithered. Lew would've been proud of me.

When I got to the three steps that led down into the living room, I could see somebody — or something — on the couch. I could hear a kind of ragged, wheezy breathing.

Then it stirred and reached for something. I wondered if its tentacles were long enough to get me. I'd just started to slide backward when I heard the clink of glass on glass, then a gurgle and splash. The mutant was having a cocktail.

"Wes?" I whispered.

The pouring stopped. "Billy, is that you?"

"What are you doing sitting in the dark?" I demanded, getting to my feet.

"Don't turn on the light!"

"Why not?"

"I've been drinking. I'm drunk."

"You don't sound drunk."

"Take my word for it."

My eyes were partly used to the dark, so I made my way toward him.

"Yuk, what's that?" I stopped in my tracks.

"What's what?"

"I stepped on something soft."

"It's probably my boot."

I was shocked. "You left your boots in the middle of the floor?"

"One boot. I couldn't get the other one off."

One boot. Right out in the middle of the floor. I knew something awful had happened.

I groped my way to the couch. "What happened?"

"You know that guy," he said, struggling a little for the words, "that you met? Michael?"

"In the wheelchair, you mean?"

I could see him nod. "Well, he died today."

"God. That's too bad."

Wes took another drink.

I leaned back just a little. I was starting to feel uneasy. The whole scene reminded me of the only times I ever saw my dad really troubled. He'd come in from having dinner with some big-time actor or director he'd known for years; he'd be high or maybe just drunk. He'd always say the same thing: that he didn't want to just teach drama, he wanted to be in the theater. Mom would listen, try to get some coffee in him, and in the middle of all that send me to bed with the don't-worry speech.

But I did worry. I felt like it was partly my fault — maybe I came along and he had to take a steady job — plus I didn't know what to do. I'd stand there in my pajamas while Dad just felt like shit.

And there I was doing it again, sitting there while Wes felt rotten. So I scooted closer on the couch. Wes had his head back, eyes closed. A few strands of hair had fallen across his forehead. For him, that was completely disheveled. I put one hand out slowly and touched his arm.

"Wha'?" he said with just the littlest slur.

"Nothing." I didn't know whether to pat, stroke, or grip. I decided to grip.

Wes reached across to cover my hand with his. "Four months ago I took the AIDS antibody test. It was negative."

"So you're fine, right? You're negative."

"I take it again in two months. If it's negative again, I'm fine."

"How could you get anything? You never go out."

"Not like I used to, that's for sure. Anyway, how do you know what I do all day? You're at the track."

"You do it in the daytime?"

"It doesn't take that long, Billy, and it doesn't have to

be dark. The point is, nobody with any brains or consideration does anything risky anymore."

"So," I said, "since you test negative and since you're smart and considerate, everything *is* fine."

"I suppose," he said with a sigh, "but this thing with Michael just pushed all my buttons. I won't know for sure for two months."

So. My dad was afraid he was wasting his life. Wes was afraid he wouldn't have a life to waste.

I moved a little closer, squeezed his forearm a little tighter. His hand closed around mine, too. We sat there for a while. I was pretty sure he didn't want me to say anything. I was glad for that. I didn't know what to say.

Then his hand left mine, drifted through the darkness, and settled on his stomach. "God, I ate a pizza. In the old days I used to always eat a pizza when I was screwed up."

"I thought you used to go shopping."

"Yeah. For pizzas."

"Why don't you go to bed. I'll help you."

"If I get up I'll puke."

"Just lie down here, then. I'll get a blanket."

"If I lie down I'll puke."

"Then I'll just keep you company."

"If you keep me company I'll puke."

"Thanks a lot."

He groped for the arm of the sofa, then lurched to his feet.

"I'll be right behind you," I shouted.

Half a minute later I had my arms around his stomach, holding him like my mom held me when I had the flu.

"Oh," he groaned, groping for the handle on the toilet. "I hate for you to see me like this."

"I'm just surprised you throw up like everybody else. Knowing you, I thought it'd come out gift-wrapped."

"Don't make me laugh." He leaned into the bowl again.

7

Tucson advertised about four hundred sunny days a year, but the next Saturday wasn't one of them, and I felt like the weather looked. It seemed to get to everybody — everybody except Moon's Medicine, who was playing around with Chicken Little and generally feeling chipper. After all, she didn't know she'd lost by a nose; she'd run her heart out.

Lew and I just clammed up and did our work while I kept an eye out for Cara Mae, as usual. I seemed to always wonder when Cara would turn up and how she'd feel when she did. One thing about her: I would never get tired of the same old thing. She was just as liable to ride away in the middle of a conversation as she was to suddenly throw her arms around my neck. I liked her, though. I liked her a lot. And for all I know I liked her partly *because* she was so impulsive, even though that worried me sometimes. I'd never known a girl like her before, that's for sure.

"Hey," said Lew as I was finishing up with some tack. "What do these bozos want?"

Fletcher and Grif were bearing down on us, and

Fletcher — the slick one — was grinning in that cruel way he had where only half his mouth moved.

"Bring out that gray," he said to me.

"What for?"

"Because she's mine now."

"Take a hike," Lew suggested.

"Fine, okay. We'll do it the hard way." He turned to his buddy. "Stay here and keep an eye on our horse. I'll be right back."

Lew and I glanced at each other, then at Grif. The guy was huge. He looked like an armadillo on steroids. His arms couldn't even hang down normally. On his right bicep was the classic Mom tattoo. Hard to believe he had a mother. He seemed like the type who'd just crawled out of the swamp and started eating trees.

"You scumbag," said Lew.

Grif didn't move. He just stood there behind those mirrored sunglasses.

"Taking somebody's horse right out from under him." Lew took a couple of steps so he was right in his face. "You big pile of shit."

Nothing. It was like taunting a house.

Lew looked over at me. "What does Fletcher do, wind this moron up every morning . . . ?"

He never got to finish. Grif just let him have it, not even a punch, but an openhanded slap that sent Lew sprawling.

"Now you're really gonna get it," said Lew, jumping to his feet. When he put his head down and charged, I did, too. Lew got his arms partway around Grif's waist and I grabbed an arm. Since neither of us died immediately, I thought we were doing okay, but the next thing I knew I was airborne. He'd tossed me like a newspaper. He had Lew's head in his other hand. I didn't know whether he was going to crush it or bowl it.

"Stop it!" Jack shouted. "That's enough!"

Lew and I picked ourselves up warily. He looked a little pale, so I must have been white as milk.

"Lew, get Moon's Medicine out of her stall."

"Goddammit, Jack."

"I just talked to the owner on the phone. It's his horse and that's the way he wants it."

"Let Fatso get her, then," Lew muttered.

"Yeah," I wheezed, trying to sound just as tough.

"This kind of help, no wonder your horses lose." Fletcher picked up a bridle. "I'll do it myself."

I'd had the breath partly knocked out of me, so I leaned against the water trough.

"You bag of bones," Fletcher snarled at Moon's Medicine, "turn around here."

We could hear her lash out with her hind legs and rattle the walls.

"And you get lost!" Out came the hen with a squawk.

Lew and I snuck a look at each other. Without Chicken Little all the Moon would do was eat and wear herself out walking in her stall.

"Thanks for helping out with Grif," Lew said as we trudged toward the parking lot.

"A lot of help I was." I remembered flying through

the air and landing on my ass. "And, anyway, I thought you knew karate and aikido and all that crap."

Lew stared down at his combat boots. "I know. But it's easier with Edgar. He stands the right way and lets me throw him. But what the hell," he said heartily. "At least we tried."

"Hey, you guys!" It was Cara Mae, running toward us with her head down so her hat wouldn't blow off. "I heard you got in a fight. What happened?"

We filled her in.

"Are you okay?" she asked me.

"Sure."

"I hope you punched that guy's lights out."

"Not exactly," I began.

"We did okay," interrupted Lew. "He won't screw around with us anymore."

"Right, I really terrorized his arm."

Cara was being extra-attentive, fussing over me and all. From behind her, Lew made an A-OK sign with his thumb and forefinger. "Meet you in the jeep," he said, taking off so we could be alone.

"I looked for you all morning," I told her.

She was rubbing my arm, kind of petting me. "I figured. But I felt so stupid after the other night I just stayed out of sight. I ought to find Abby and apologize, I guess. And Lew, too." She was looking everywhere but at me. "And you," she added softly.

"That's okay. We're all used to you."

"But still. I'm kind of a pain in the ass. I don't know why you guys even put up with me."

"We like you. I mean they do, Abby and Lew. And me, too. I like you."

Then she looked at me intently. "Do you really?"

"Uh-huh."

"No matter what? Even when I act crazy?"

"You're impulsive," I said, "and passionate."

"You think I'm that?"

"Impulsive?"

"The other one."

"Sure. You've got really strong feelings."

"Or they've got me," she said ruefully.

"You know, I kind of envy that sometimes."

"You're kidding. You mean you'd want to go off half-cocked?"

"I'm just such an average kid."

"Oh, Billy, you're not. You're way better than average. You're dependable and thoughtful and solid. That's why I like you. You're something steady I can hold on to."

I looked away from her eyes, which were locked onto mine.

"I thought we'd say this to each other somewhere else, at night or in a restaurant with a candle, maybe."

"Can you pick me up later?"

"I don't know if I can get the car."

"Try, okay? I'll be out by the mailbox at nine."

"Tonight's the night, man," said Lew as we drove up Old Nuevo. "I saw the way she kissed you goodbye. I thought your pants were going to catch on fire."

"Well, if that's true, then I'm scared."

118

"Don't let her know that. Act like you know the score."

"Maybe I'll wear a red smoking jacket."

"Don't worry. It'll be great."

"What if Cara's a virgin?"

"You know," he said, tugging on his ripped T-shirt so the holes were in the right places, "she could be. You're the first guy who ever got anywhere with her. At least that I know of."

"Talk about the blind leading the blind."

"Don't worry so much about it. Just do what comes naturally."

"In that case, I'll jerk off."

He pulled up in front of the house. A plain white van was parked beside Wes's fancy green one.

"Just think," he said, idly rubbing his earring, "the next time I see you, you won't be Billy the Kid anymore. You'll be a man."

"I'd settle for being taller."

"Pardner, if screwing made people taller, we'd be a nation of giants."

Inside, Wes was sitting at his PC. He whipped off his reading glasses as soon as I came in.

"I saw that."

"Saw what?"

"The glasses."

"I don't see any glasses. Maybe you ought to have your eyes checked."

Then we grinned at each other.

"Who's here?" I asked, looking around.

"Just us chickens. Why?"

"Then whose van is that?"

"I thought you'd never ask." He picked up some keys, then dangled them at arm's length.

"I don't get it."

"It's yours."

"The van?"

He tossed them to me. "Until the end of August. Six weeks."

"You're kidding!"

"Yes, so give those keys back. Of course I'm not kidding."

"Wow, I don't know what to say."

" 'Thank you a million times' might be nice."

"Thank you . . ."

"Oh, please. I was just kidding. The fact is it was so easy I couldn't pass it up. Starting in September that van belongs to the shop, but when the Chevy dealer called me and said it was in now, I had them bring it out here."

I turned the keys over and over, watching them glitter in the light. A car of my own. "I'll be real careful."

"I know you will; that's one of the reasons you can have it. There's not a nick anywhere on my van, and believe me, I've looked." He put his arm around my shoulders and led me outdoors. "Now I need a couple of things for dinner. Mind driving down to the market for them?"

I grinned up at him, still fooling with the keys, turning them over and over in my hand like a magic charm.

"What about your folks?" he asked as I fumbled with the lock. "Do you want them to know?"

"Dad, maybe," I said, opening the door and peering inside. "I'm not so sure about Mom." I climbed in, adjusted the seat and the mirrors.

"One more secret," Wes said, leaning in the open window. "That antibody test I talked about the other night is between you and me. Your folks don't even have to know. There's nothing they can do and I don't want them to worry." He put out his hand and I shook it. "Okay?" he said.

"Okay."

When I picked Cara Mae up by the mailbox she said, "Another new car?"

"Not exactly, but it's mine for a while, so we can go anywhere any time we want."

"Unless my dad grounds me."

"Why would he do that?" I eased us off the road and, putting the van in low, crawled up the hill to the place we always parked.

"Aw, I just took a shower and put on a clean T-shirt so I'll smell good for you and he thinks I'm gonna come home pregnant."

"That's not going to happen."

"Yeah? That's what they all say."

I took my hand off her shoulder. Cara shook her head. "Sorry, that just jumped out."

I put my hand back and she pressed one cheek against it. "So, how'd you get this car?"

"I think God's on my side. Wes bought it for the shop, but he doesn't need it right now so he's letting me use it."

She turned to me and the brims of our hats, like big beaks, touched. "Do you believe in God?"

"I guess so."

"Some guy on the radio says God sees every little thing and never forgets."

"Makes God sound like an elephant with a telescope."

"Do you ever pray?" she asked, grinning.

I shook my head.

"Me neither. I used to all the time, for things to be different and for nice clothes and for my mom to come back, but nothing ever happened, so I stopped."

"When I was about nine, my folks took me to a bunch of different churches and said I could pick one if I wanted. I was pretty young, but none of them really turned me on."

"Your parents sound cool."

"They are. My uncle is, too."

She scooted closer to me. "What's it like living with a gay guy?"

"Like living with anybody else, I guess."

"It doesn't feel funny?"

"A little. But my dad explained things to me a long time ago. He told me about Wes."

She took out a joint, offered it to me, then lit up. In the glow of the lighter her skin was beautiful.

"He didn't say it was bad or anything like that?"

"No, never. So when I got older and started to hear all that fag and fruit stuff, it didn't make a lot of sense."

"Did you say anything?" she asked, inhaling deeply.

I shook my head. "I was afraid of getting my butt kicked or afraid they'd call me names, too. I guess I'm not very brave."

"Bullshit, it was smart to keep quiet. Whose mind were you going to change, anyway? Besides, you fought Grif, and nobody fights Grif. He broke some guy's neck once."

"Oh, great."

Cara Mae flicked the end off her joint, put the rest away, then tipped her hat back till it fell into the seat behind her. Then she leaned toward me, took my hat off, and threw it in the back. "Is sex bad, do you think?" she asked, playing with my hair.

"No."

"Me neither," she said, closing her eyes.

I don't mean to say it was like in some movies where people's clothes float away like labels off wet jars, but after the stuck zippers, the hundreds of buttons, the catches and hooks, we did go further faster than we ever had before. And not just further and faster but harder, too.

Cara grabbed me like she was panic-shifting an eighteen-wheeler, then jerked her hand away and pulled on my hair. I touched her all over, thinking, *So that's what a girl feels like.*

"Billy," she panted, chewing her cinnamon-flavored Trident a mile a minute, "are we about to do it here?"

"We can't. I don't have anything. You know, so you won't get pregnant." I'd given up carrying the condoms everywhere I went.

"Oh, man." She leaned back in the seat, looking exhausted. "Seems like all my life I've been saying no. And now that it's yes, *you're* saying no."

"My uncle's going away tomorrow," I said quickly. "So we could use the house then. It'd be nicer than in a car, anyway."

"You mean do it in a bed?"

"Sure."

Shyly she began to fasten her belt. "Should I bring anything?"

"Maybe Fritos and dip."

She started to giggle, then stopped dressing, letting me see for another few seconds her pretty skin. "I love it when you make me laugh."

"Is anybody going to know?" Cara Mae asked, peering out the side window as we pulled into the drive.

"Neighbors?"

"Uh-huh." She looked around cautiously.

"I'll tell Wes we came by so I could pick up some money."

"Would he care, do you think?"

"Only if we weren't careful."

"My dad'd care."

"Your dad's asleep," I said as we got out of the car, and she laughed.

When I opened the front door, I let Cara go first.

"This is beautiful!"

"My uncle's got good taste to burn."

"I'm gonna take my boots off. I'd feel terrible if I got

something dirty." She backed out onto the top step, beat some dust out of her jeans with her hat, then kicked off her old Justins. One of them had a good-sized hole in the bottom and when she saw how dirty the bottom of her sock was she took it off, too.

"Want something to drink?" I asked as she padded around with one bare foot.

"I'm okay."

"You could smoke a joint if you want."

She shook her head and grinned. "Not today."

"Seven-up?"

"I'd belch." She picked up one of the hard-on statuettes. "Is this some gay thing?"

"Hood ornament."

"Bullshit," she said, laughing.

"Actually, it's some kind of Indian fertility symbol."

"For crops or babies?"

"Crops, I think."

"Do you want to have babies?" she asked, coming toward the bar, where I was trying to look casual.

"I'd rather have crops."

She gave me a look.

"Someday, I guess. Do you?"

"I don't know. I have enough trouble just taking care of myself."

"Want to see the bedroom?" I blurted. Wonderful. She says how tough her life is, so I invite her into the bedroom.

"Sure," she said. "That's what we came for."

We walked down the hall as slowly as people in a

museum. We looked at the framed prints and even glanced into the bathroom.

"This is it." The bed looked enormous all of a sudden.

We sat down together and bounced a little, like people buying a mattress. I knew we couldn't keep bouncing forever, though, so I put my hand on her shoulder.

"What's your room at home like?" she asked abruptly.

I took my hand away. "Uh, you know. Not this nice, but okay. Big picture of Larry Bird I'm going to take down. To hell with those tall guys; I'll get me a poster with a jockey on it. How about yours?"

"Just a room," she said with a shrug. "I don't ever paint or put stuff up 'cause I know we're just gonna move on."

"Can I take your other sock off?"

"Sure."

Cara Mae fell back and put one leg up in the air. I slipped her white anklet off, folded it neatly, and put it on the floor. Then I leaned over and kissed her on the ankle.

"What are you doing down there?"

"Well, since I usually kiss you on the lips first, this being a special day and all, I thought I'd start at the other end."

Cara laughed once — a nervous little whoosh — then got serious just as quick.

"What's wrong?" I asked.

"I don't like to think of you in your room back there in Missouri and me in mine out here."

"I know. But I'm here now."

She nodded, bit her lower lip and frowned, then began to unbutton her blouse. "I wish I had bigger boobs."

"I don't care."

"Then you're the only guy in the world that doesn't. All you ever hear is boobs, boobs, boobs."

"Wrong. All you ever hear is tall, tall, tall. Does anybody ever say 'short, dark, and handsome'?"

She stared down at her lap and the crumpled bra she'd dropped there.

"Hey," I said, "your chest is blushing."

"C'mon, greenhorn. You take something off now."

"Sure, okay." I got down to my underpants. "Now your jeans, please."

"Give me a hand here."

I took hold of the cuffs and pulled. "Whew. Luckily, one of the neighbors has a winch on his jeep. I'll just back that up here and we'll have these off in a jiffy."

"Pull harder!"

"How do you get these on by yourself?"

"I set the alarm fifteen minutes early."

Then I folded her Levi's and sheepishly slipped out of my shorts. "Maybe we should get under the covers," I said.

As she pulled back the peach comforter I took the condom out of the drawer of the nightstand. "We'll have to use this."

"I know."

I slipped in beside her. "Lew said not to tell you this, but it's my first time."

"Me too."

"Don't worry. It'll be okay."

"I'm not gonna say that's what they all say."

"Thanks."

Making love was a little strange at first. I'd never worn a condom before so I felt like part of me was dressed for scuba diving. We were both pretty bony and awkward, but I think we did okay for amateurs.

The thing I liked most, though, wasn't the sex itself; it was afterward, when we both fell asleep for a little while. I liked waking up and being in bed with Cara Mae, having her beside me.

I thought of my folks, who slept together every night. It sounded great. Then there was my uncle, who always slept alone; Lew and Abby, who never got to sleep together; Cara Mae's dad by himself in his rented house.

I'm sure being on your own, sleeping alone, and waking up alone isn't the worst thing in the world, but waking up warm as bread and a little woozy and satisfied with somebody you really like just has to be the best.

Cara whimpered and turned to me. She put one hand up and felt her nose.

"Did I snore?"

"No."

"I dreamt I did."

"It wouldn't have mattered."

"You've never heard me snore."

"I'll be right back. I'm going to get something."

"What?"

"You'll see." I slipped out of bed and picked up my pants.

"Don't," she said. "You're cute naked."

It was my turn to blush all over. I dashed out of the room. As I walked through the house barefoot, though, I felt good. Everything looked a little different: sharper, crisper around the edges, brighter. Is that how men always see things compared to boys? I wondered. Or does jerking off hurt your eyesight, while intercourse restores it?

"Champagne?" she asked when I bought back a bottle and two glasses.

"Martinelli's sparkling apple juice."

"That's fine."

I had Wes's zillion-dollar champagne flutes.

"Beats the hell out of Dixie cups," said Cara Mae as I poured.

"I don't know what to say or what to drink to exactly, except I'm glad we're here together."

"That's nice," she said, touching glasses.

We sat propped up in bed with the covers more or less over us; we sipped and stared at the picture of the lips.

"I'm glad you're not gay," she said.

"I'm glad you're not, too, or we wouldn't be here."

"Could you sleep some more?" she asked suddenly.

"Now?"

"Uh-huh. I was awake half the night worrying about today: would you like it, would you like me, would I do it right, would I snore."

"I was worried too," I said, sliding down in the bed.

"Abby says you never forget the first time, not the person or the place or . . ."

"The apple juice?"

"Yeah." She grinned sleepily. "Or the apple juice."

Wes was making breakfast when I came into the kitchen carrying my boots, my hat, and my T-shirt.

"Remember when you wouldn't go out in the sun without two inches of goo all over you?"

I looked down at my brown arms and chest as I slipped the shirt on. "Remember when I wouldn't wear anything but striped shirts?"

"You're about to need another pair of boots." He eyed the Tony Lamas he'd given me. "We'll get you some before you go home."

Before you go home. Two months ago that might have been okay. Now it didn't sound so inviting.

"Does that van of yours need an oil change or anything?" he asked, putting down a plate of bacon and scrambled eggs.

"Gee, no. We don't drive around much."

"How goes the summer romance, anyway?"

Was that what it was? Was that *all* it was? "Okay, I guess."

"I had one of those once. I was in graduate school here taking some anthropology classes. They were easy, he was cute, and there wasn't anything to do but eat Mexican food and fool around."

"What was his name?"

He shook his head. "I can't even remember."

I wondered if I would ever tell anyone there was this girl in Tucson when I'd been sixteen but her name escaped me. That seemed impossible.

"What's different in here?" I said after a couple of mouthfuls.

"Too many jalapeños?"

"Not in the eggs, in the room." I looked around carefully. "Ha! What happened to the Snoopy phone?"

"Oh, I got rid of it. That was just kitsch. Something to show I didn't sleep with *Architectural Digest*."

I checked the new white one. Naturally it was some top-of-the-line model with a hundred buttons. All of a sudden it rang.

"See," Wes quipped, "sensitive, too. If you talk about it, it talks back. Go ahead and answer it."

It was my mom, so I pulled up one of the bar stools and put on my hat like she could see the new me.

"I'm fine," I said. "No, Wes is here. Yeah, he's fine, too."

He patted me on the shoulder as he passed behind me with a plate.

"We got all your cards," she said. "It looks interesting out there."

"It is. It's great."

"Your dad and I want to come sometime. We'll all go. To see Wes."

What a funny idea, to go and come back again. Would Cara Mae be here? Would I introduce her to my parents? As what? A friend?

"I guess I really called because I miss you," Mom said softly.

"I miss you, too." It was true, even though I'd been busy and I hadn't thought much about Bradleyville or my folks. But that didn't mean I couldn't miss them just the same.

"All the back-to-school sales are on. I bought you some socks and underwear yesterday at Boys' World."

Naturally Mom didn't know everything about Cara and me. To her I was still the little kid she had to buy shorts for. How would she feel if she knew I took off my underpants, dropped them on the floor with my boots, and climbed into bed with a girl?

"How's Dad?" I asked.

"Busy. You know how he hates summer school, but it's almost over." She took a breath and let it out. "I better go, Sugar. I know Daddy sends you his love, and I do, too. I'm real anxious to see you."

"Me too. 'Bye."

"Everything okay?" asked Wes after I sat there for a few seconds.

"Sure, I just . . . I don't know exactly."

Just then the phone rang again.

"That thing loves you," Wes said, turning on the tap.

"It's me," said Lew. "Can you give me a ride this morning?"

"Sure. What's wrong, trouble in the motor pool?"

"Edgar's bent out of shape because I won't go on maneuvers with him today, so no wheels."

"I'll be right over."

"Wait a second," he said. "He just screwed up my day. Let's screw up his."

"Why?"

"Are you kidding? That's what Edgar and I do. He puts the hum on me, I put it on him. So just listen."

I strolled up to Lew's front door whistling, just like we'd planned. I knocked, waited, then stepped inside.

Lew's dad dropped from the ceiling. He had a knife in one hand, a machine gun in the other, and he was screaming at the top of his lungs. I could see right down his throat, we were that close.

As soon as he ran out of breath I said, "Hi, Mr. Coley."

He took a step back. For once he wasn't wearing makeup, and I could see he was a pretty good-looking guy.

"I'm recommending a field-grade commission for bravery," he said. "You are now a lieutenant."

"Thanks."

"Fall in. I'll take the point."

I followed him down the hall. He leaped through every doorway, machine gun leveled. He fired a few rounds of blanks into the TV room, glancing at me cunningly. I never flinched.

"A typical mutant hideout," I said.

He narrowed his eyes. "Precisely, Captain."

"If this keeps up, I can retire and draw a pension by the time we get to the guest bathroom."

He grinned. "Humor is commendable. It keeps the men's morale up."

In the kitchen Lew was finishing breakfast. His mom was at the sink again, this time wearing a Walkman headset. She swayed slightly as she scrubbed in slow motion.

Lew and I nodded, avoiding each other's eyes so we didn't crack up and blow the whole thing.

"Sub-private Coley. Here is a man with ice water in his veins," said Lew's dad.

I glanced his way. "Sub-private?"

"Less than the least," said Lew.

"Cool under fire," Edgar chanted, "nerves of steel, quick to make decisions and stand by them. A model soldier."

"Can I have your autograph, Billy?" Lew said.

"Captain Kennedy to you, Sub-private. Now let's move out."

As Lew reached for his things, his dad darted toward the sink, kissed his wife on the cheek, and disappeared out the back door. Lew and I exchanged high fives and snickered.

"When we get outside," he whispered, "he's going to set off a couple of explosions and spray us with blanks."

Sure enough, not two steps out the door all hell broke loose. We strolled through flying dirt and smoke like we were on our way to church.

Lew and I laughed for a couple of blocks.

"Dad'll make you a five-star general after that performance," he said. "You were great, man."

"If you hadn't told me what to expect I'd be changing my pants. He dropped down from the ceiling like a panther."

"He was braced up there like a rock climber for about ten minutes. That sonofabitch is strong, I'll say that for him."

"He really gets into it."

"You're telling me."

"Do you think he loves your mom?"

"Come again?"

I repeated the question.

"I don't know. He must have, once."

"Do you love Abby?"

"What is all this?"

"I don't know for sure. Do you? Just tell me if you love Abby."

He shook his head. "No. We like each other, but like now, she's been in L.A. all week. Who knows what she's been doing." For a block or so he searched in all six pockets of his fatigue pants for some gum. "So am I going to hear your side of this? Does your dad love your mom?"

"Sure."

"And do you love Cara Mae?"

"I don't know. I'll be gone in a month."

"Better make hay while the sun shines."

"I suppose."

"I'll tell you this. If the Russkies don't press the big red button by September, I'm in deep shit."

"Why?"

"Are you kidding? The track closes down, Abby and

her dad van their horses to Turf Paradise, all the exercise girls take off, and you go back to Dinkyville."

"Bradleyville."

"Whatever. Man, I'll be working at McDonald's and all the guys I almost graduated with will be in college." He took off his fatigue hat with Almost a Ghost scrawled on its bill and stared at it as I turned into the track and showed the guard my stable pass.

"Billy," Abby yelled, getting out of her daddy's Cadillac, "how goes it?"

"Okay. How was L.A.?"

"*Fab*ulous." She put her arms around me for a hello hug. "Cara says you guys have been cashing some tickets."

"Yeah, but I'm still afraid to bet more than six dollars at a time."

"Guess who went to Disneyland?" She pointed to her Mickey Mouse T-shirt.

"You?" I guessed, playing along.

"And my dad."

I tried to picture her father in the old Magic Kingdom, but couldn't. Not even in Frontierland.

"Where's Lew?"

"Round back."

"Did I say Cara's busy and wants you to wait for her?"

"Uh-uh."

"Well, she does. By the way, her complexion looks better already."

"Whose does?"

"Cara's," she said mischievously.

"I don't get it."

"You never heard how sex is good for your complexion?"

"God, Abby," I said, blushing again.

"I love to see you do that," she exclaimed. "Makes me feel about ten years old. And speaking of rosy cheeks, I better find Lew and see if he still loves me."

I watched her turn the corner by Jack's office. Abby was barely nineteen, not even three years older than me, and even though she talked about Disneyland like a kid, I still felt like her little brother most of the time.

Cara was nowhere in sight, so when Chicken Little walked up, I got the idea of visiting Moon's Medicine. I'd seen Fletcher and Grif drive away in their pickup, so I knew there wouldn't be anybody around.

"Want to go?" I asked the hen, picking her up.

The good barns — meaning moderately successful with their stock — were up close to the racing secretary's office and the main track. The rest of us were arranged accordingly. Jack was somewhere just below the middle, but Fletcher and Grif were almost at the bottom. They had only three or four stalls in one of the oldest parts of the backstretch. Jack didn't have fancy awnings or real flowers like some of the big outfits, but he did have his initials up and Lew and I kept the place clean. Fletcher and Grif didn't have a name or a number or a brand, just two or three depressed-looking nags standing with their behinds to the outdoors, staring at the walls.

Nobody was around, so I was talking to the chicken. "Where's the Moon, huh? Wanna see your old pal?"

I figured she was in the last stall, so I knocked jauntily,

put the hen on the ledge of the Dutch door, and looked in.

"What are you doing lying down, you big loafer?" I nudged the chicken, who flew off the ledge and into the stall. "Look who's here," I said.

When Moon's Medicine didn't even look up, much less haul herself onto all fours, I started to get a cold feeling in my gut.

"Hey!" I pounded the frame with my hand.

When I opened the door, the chicken scuttled out. I just stood there for a second. Then I knelt down and put my hand on the big gray neck. Cold.

"Oh, shit," I said as I stood up and took a step backward.

Cara Mae was beating on the dashboard with her hat, and every time she hit it, she swore. "Goddammit, goddammit, goddammit!"

She'd been carrying on most of the way home, and when I'd reached to comfort her she knocked my hand away like a guy in a bar who was looking for trouble.

"We should get those guys," she said, "and put the hurt on 'em bad."

"I know, but take it easy."

"Take it easy? They killed Moon's Medicine! Why should I take it easy?"

"Jack says it was probably a heart attack."

"Jack says, Jack says. Jack doesn't know."

"Horses die, Cara Mae. Bad as they are, Fletcher and Grif didn't have her long enough to really mistreat her. She didn't starve to death. And there was no reason to shoot her full of drugs, because she wasn't even entered in a race."

"Don't you get it?" she insisted as I turned onto Shadow Road. "She died 'cause she was tired of being passed around like an ugly stepchild. She'd had it with that shit. Nobody really wanted her, so she just gave up. That's what happened."

I looked out the front window. Two hundred yards away, behind some oleanders, was the house I'd never seen. "No matter what I say you're going to bite my head off."

"Maybe I am, because you don't know nothin' about nothin'." She barged out, slamming the door so hard I winced.

More from habit than anything else I drove up the hill, following the ruts we'd made, and parked looking out over Tucson.

It was so different in the daytime. Down below, the roads were full of cars going to the office or the mall. Naturally I couldn't see the lights of people's houses, just the roofs and sometimes the glint of their windows. Inside they were watching TV or vacuuming or taking showers.

I climbed out and sat on the front bumper. Off in the distance I could see Tucson General Hospital. Probably some people in there had died, too. And their friends were feeling worse than me — more sad, more confused. Did those souls mingle with Moon's Medicine's like the smoke from separate campfires? What happened after you died, anyway — anything? Nothing?

I heard footsteps behind me. "I thought you might be up here," Cara Mae said tentatively.

"I didn't know where else to go."

"Sorry about before."

I shrugged. "That's okay." I rolled up the sleeves of my shirt, an already faded denim one with pearl snaps. It was hard to believe that my strong brown arms would get cold someday and not be able to move.

"Are you mad?" She moved around so her hat blocked the sun for me.

I squinted up at her. "I'm the one who found Moon's Medicine."

"I heard it was Grif."

"Jack told me to shut up about it and let somebody else stumble onto her. He said it'd look suspicious, since she'd been taken away from us."

"Why didn't you tell me?"

"Didn't have much chance, did I. You were carrying on."

"I felt bad."

"You felt mad is what you felt. And I was afraid if I told you the whole story I'd start in crying again."

"When were you crying?"

"After I found her and before I told Jack. I couldn't help myself." I could feel it start all over — the tight throat, the tears hot behind my eyes. "But I was afraid you'd think I was a sissy."

She put her arms around me. "I wouldn't."

"Well, you didn't cry; you just beat the crap out of your hat."

"Maybe I wanted to and I couldn't."

"I did enough for both of us." I was trying hard, but one big one leaked out anyway. I could still see Moon's Medicine laid out, her legs bent like she was running.

Cara Mae pulled my face into her stomach. "It's okay. I don't think you're a sissy. I just think I'm a jerk. I shouldn't ever say anything about anything unless I'm on a horse. I don't think straight with my feet on solid ground."

"You're so lucky," I said, wiping my eyes with my sleeve.

She gave a little snort of disbelief. "Me? Why am I lucky?"

"Because you know what you want to be. I don't have a clue anymore."

"You don't want to be a vet?"

"All they do is watch sore horses walk and give shots."

"That's just the bottom-of-the-barrel types that work here. Good ones operate and everything."

I shook my head. "I couldn't do that."

"Could you be a trainer?"

I took a breath and let it out. "My folks would just about pass out."

She rubbed my shoulder absently. "I never thought I was lucky before."

"Well, you are. You're not going to waste a lot of time trying one thing, then another, then another." I thought of my dad coming home a little drunk. "And you're not going to settle for something close, either. You'll have the real, exact thing."

"Hell, all I ever heard before was 'aspiring below her

142

true potential' and 'about as much self-esteem as a shoe.' "

"Who said that?"

"Oh, some counselor at some school somewhere."

"Forget that," I said. "I'd give a lot to feel like you do."

She took off her hat and mine, then put her arms around me again. For a minute we didn't say anything.

"Tell me some more," she whispered finally.

"About Moon's Medicine?"

She shook her head. "About how lucky I am."

9

"You can always tell it's August," said Lew, "when you see those." He pointed south toward the towering banks of clouds.

"I thought it never rained in the desert."

"Well, it rains in August." He poured a cup of water over his head, then shook it off like an Irish setter. "Fucking August. I thought it'd never come."

"Me neither."

"What a summer, though, huh?" He grinned.

"Don't talk like it's over. There's a whole month yet."

"Not really. There's only twenty-seven days to the Tucson Derby, and that's the end as far as we're concerned."

"Okay, almost a whole month, then."

"Abby's already talking about going back to the Coast."

"And Cara's talking about another semester of torture in Phoenix."

"Hey!" shouted Jack. "You guys! Go on down to where the big horse vans pull in and find me a filly named The Dark Mirage." He waved some paper and Lew jogged that way.

Automatically I picked up a bridle and a lead chain

and started out. I remembered when I hadn't been able to tell a halter from a bridle, a curry comb from a scraper. Once I'd been scared to death of horses; now I knew enough to feel my way down a stallion's front leg and find the heat that meant he needed a little time in an ice bucket. I could even reach into a horse's mouth, grab his tongue, and tie it down with a yard or so of gauze if he was the type that'd choke on it once he got to running.

"Remember how the Moon'd just stick out her tongue so you could get to it easy?" I asked.

"She was a great old horse," Lew agreed. He pointed toward the knot of handlers who'd gathered at the back of the van. "Speaking of Moon's Medicine, there's the killers now."

Fletcher and Grif were talking to some other guys, or at least Fletcher was talking, every now and then glancing at the truck driver who was setting up a ramp for the horses.

"Well, now," Fletcher said as we walked past, "look who's here. The punk and the pipsqueak."

"Up yours," we said in unison.

"You boys down here to collect something else with a myocardial infarction so you can pass it along just before it dies?"

"Hey, you stole that horse from Jack, and you know it."

"Listen, Coley, Jack had an owner wasn't satisfied with the way his stock was being cared for, and I was willing to see what I could do with some of his damaged goods. It just happened to be too late for me to use my training skills."

145

"You couldn't train a dog to eat meat."

A horse clattered down the ramp. But nobody stepped up to claim it, because things were heating up.

"And I suppose you can, you and your earring."

"Yeah, as a matter of fact we can."

"Relax, Lew," I said. "This guy isn't worth getting hot about."

"I don't want to relax. He's all show and no go."

Fletcher took some money out of his pocket and glanced at it.

"You feel like puttin' some of this where your mouth is?"

"Any day, tube steak."

"What are you boys down here to collect?"

I looked at the papers. "Three-year-old filly named The Dark Mirage."

"I've got a three-year-old in there just shipped down from Prescott. Name's French Bred and I've never laid eyes on her. Five hundred dollars says my filly can beat yours." He thrust the bills right at us: five of them, all hundreds, all as crisp as if he'd made them himself.

"You got a bet," snapped Lew.

"Hold it, hold it," I whispered. "Do you just happen to have five hundred dollars on you?"

"We'll get it," he hissed.

"I can give y'all a day," Fletcher drawled, "to bust your piggy banks and count up all your pennies."

The other guys chuckled.

"Who'll hold the money?" Lew demanded.

One of the racetrack guards who'd been leaning on

the van said he would. "You guys give me your five by tomorrow this time or Fletcher here gets his money back and the bet's off."

"And if that happens," Fletcher said menacingly, "you snotnoses will shut your mouths, and I mean for good. Understand?" On cue, Grif shuffled forward.

"We'll have the money," Lew said, looking at me.

Maybe Fletcher and Grif hadn't really done anything to Moon's Medicine, but she'd died in their barn. Maybe revenge wasn't a noble motive, but I saw the chance to get back at them. I took a deep breath and let it out. "I don't know if Jack'll go for a match race, Fletcher."

"Don't need a match race. This horse of yours is a maiden, ain't she? Well, so's mine. We'll just find ourselves a maiden race, enter 'em both, and the winner gets the five hundred."

"The winner of the race?" I asked innocently.

"Forget the goddamn race," Fletcher barked. "Maybe there's ten other horses that night. It don't matter. What matters is your horse against mine, that's all. We run last and second-to-last, one of us still gets beat and the other gets the money."

"Back off, Fletcher," said the guard who'd volunteered to hold the thousand dollars. "It's just a little bet with a couple of kids."

Fletcher jerked his arm away. "All right, all right. I'm just sick of bein' called a killer and a crappy trainer, is all." Then he turned to the driver of the van. "Well, numbnuts, let's go. Let's see what we got here."

147

The first couple of horses down belonged to other handlers. Lew and I leaned on the fence and acted casual. *Acted* is the key word.

Then a chestnut filly came halfway down the ramp, hesitated, and looked our way. Her coat was glossy and her ears were up.

"All right," said Lew, taking a step forward.

"That's not her," I whispered, grabbing at his T-shirt. "The papers say she's got a blaze and two white stockings."

Grif shambled up and took hold of the bridle as Fletcher grinned.

"Hold on," he said to his buddy. "Let's see what the competition looks like."

Lew and I snuck a look at each other, and I wiped my hands on my jeans. *Five hundred dollars.*

"Oh, man," Lew groaned as the last one was led out.

To begin with, she wasn't very big, easily a couple of hands under French Bred. But the real bad news was that she was blindfolded.

"Don't tell me they're going to lead her over to the wall, give her one last cigarette, and shoot her."

Lew shook his head. "It means she's been acting up bad."

"By the way," Fletcher bragged, "starting now I'm taking all side bets. Pass the word around."

The van driver motioned for us. "Take a good hold here," he said. "We couldn't hardly get her in the goddam van, but the trip probably took a lot of that out of her."

I wrapped the lead around my hand twice. "Are you sure?"

"No," he said, whipping the folded towel away.

She went right up on her hind legs and then fell over, taking me with her.

I remember Lew yelling, "Don't let go, Billy! Hold on!"

But that's the last I remember.

"You okay?" Cara Mae asked as I sat on a bench outside the Moon's old stall with Abby and Lew.

"I think so."

"You just got the wind knocked out of you."

"She missed kicking me in the head by about that much." I measured with my thumb and index finger.

"She's got a lot of get-up-and-go," said Lew.

"Uh-huh. Just like you've got a lot of balls betting five hundred dollars we don't have."

"No sweat," he said, nervously straightening his Dying Generation cap. "Abby'll lend it to me."

"Honey, if the world was going to end tomorrow, which it isn't, and money wasn't good for nothin', I still wouldn't give you five hundred dollars to bet on that thing in there."

Lew looked toward the stall where The Dark Mirage stood backed into a corner, every now and then lashing out with one hind foot.

"Jack," Lew said, running up to him, "this new filly is a beauty."

"I heard," Jack replied dryly, "she likes to travel in a

blindfold." He turned to me. "I also heard you got stomped on."

"Just dragged." I put my hat back on, but it didn't seem to fit. Had I bent my head?

Jack patted me on the shoulder, then walked over to the open Dutch door and took a look in. "Easy, girl," he said automatically. "Take it easy now."

"Any part of that five hundred you want," announced Lew, "you can have it."

"Thanks, I'll keep that in mind."

"Look," Abby advised, "just tell those old boys that you made a mistake. They'll understand."

"Nope," Jack said. "A bet's a bet."

"I wouldn't tell those hand-jobs I'd made a mistake for all the money in the world," Lew said. Then he turned to me. "How about your uncle?"

I shook my head. "He's no gambler, he told me so."

Cara moved some hair to one side and looked at my forehead. "That'll be black and blue tomorrow."

"Wonderful."

"I think I can come up with two hundred," she said thoughtfully, "but that's a long way from five."

"I guess I can get two hundred more."

"Where from?" Lew asked.

"I've got some money saved for college."

"Don't use that. We'll get it somewhere."

"Where?"

"I can get fifty by kicking my dad's butt arm wrestling."

"But can you do it ten times in a row before tomorrow?"

150

"Anyway," said Cara Mae edgily, "I'm using my high school money."

"That's different," Lew said.

"Like hell. Besides, we're not gonna lose."

"We're not?" Lew stared at her.

"Fletcher and Grif put that filly outside like an advertisement. I saw her on the way over here. She's not that hot."

"She just rode seven hundred miles and didn't turn a hair," Jack observed.

"So she can van like a heifer. Who cares? She's common. Go take a look at her if you don't believe me."

"We did take a look at her, Cara Mae," Lew said.

"Not close enough, then. She's just like a used car: all on the outside."

"But this one we've got is mean."

"I think she's scared is all. Probably she wasn't broke right or handled right or anything else right, so she's got some bad habits. But she's smart, I can see that in her eyes. And she's not carrying any fat."

"She has run twice in a month," Jack ventured. "I've got the form on her." He shook his head. "But she run every direction except straight."

"Look," said Cara Mae. "You're such a bunch of gloomy SOBs. There's twenty-seven days to the race, right?"

"We can take all twenty-seven if we want," I said.

"So we take the limit and run closing day. That means she can work out five times easy. We get her settled down, feed her good, and who knows what she'll show us."

"You ask me," said Abby, "she'll show us how to throw a rider and run off. But that don't mean I can't spare fifty dollars of my own money."

Lew grinned at her as she took his arm roughly, shaking her head in that way that means *I must be nuts to do this*.

"It's not going to be easy," Jack said, "to find somebody to work her in the mornings. Story's already out how she'll just eat your lunch, and most everybody's betting against her, anyway."

"Put me up, Jack." Cara Mae turned toward him, then wavered like a compass needle in the shaky hand of a lost traveler. Her eyes finally met his. "Please."

Jack took off his hat and arranged his twenty-seven hairs for a while. "Do one thing I don't want you to, get contrary on me at all, and you're off. Agreed?"

"Yes, sir."

"I mean it, Cara Mae."

"I know." She stuck out her hand.

Jack took it and they shook firmly. Once.

"Too bad," Wes said when I came into the house that evening. "You just missed your dad."

"Does he want me to call him back?"

Wes shook his head. "Everything's fine. He wanted to talk to me, anyway. We had a nice chat."

"Uh, Wes . . ."

"Are you going to want dinner tonight? Suzette and I are going out."

"No, it's okay. Cara and I have a date." I looked down at my feet. "Wes, I sort of need . . ."

"She thought you were cute, by the way."

"Who did?"

"Suzette. You met her in the shop when she was with Michael."

"I remember." I followed him into the kitchen. "Wes, you know that money you've been saving for me?"

He took a plate out of the dishwasher and inspected it. "What about it?" he asked absently.

"I sort of need two hundred dollars of it."

"Sort of?" He turned around so we were face to face. He was wearing a black silk shirt and some kind of soft pants. He'd been cleaning up but there wasn't a spot on him. I was dirty and bruised. "What happened to your head?"

"A horse dragged me."

"And the two hundred is so he won't drag you so far next time?"

"Lew and I got in a little trouble. We bet a lot of money we don't have."

"You can't just get out of it?"

"Wes, the whole backstretch knows. I wouldn't feel right backing out."

"We aren't doing some macho Code of the West thing, are we?"

"No. Lew shot off his mouth, but those guys were asking for it." I kicked at the spotless parquet tile. "Anyway, Lew and I are buddies."

"Why is it I want to sing 'Stand by Your Man'?"

"Cara says we can win."

He folded the towel he was using and draped it on the rung.

"It's your money, kiddo. Your *college* money."

"Don't remind me."

"When do you need this?"

"In the morning, I'm afraid."

"What did we ever do without the magic of the twenty-four-hour automated teller."

"Do my folks have to know?"

"Not if you don't want them to."

"Okay. Then I don't."

"You should see this place in the winter," said Cara as I parked the van right under the neon sign that said La Fuente.

"Crowded?"

"Just like Phoenix. Snowbirds from here to the Rincons and all of 'em driving Cadillacs."

"You'll have a Cadillac someday," I said.

"Bullshit."

"No, really. You know as much about horses as Jack."

"Maybe, but I'm a girl."

"So what? I went past and took a look at French Bred on my way home. I think you're right. She is common. But I wouldn't have seen it unless you told me what to look for."

She took my hand in both of hers and squeezed. "We've got to figure out what'll calm The Dark Mirage down."

I opened the restaurant's humongous door, big enough to keep out all of Santa Ana's troops. "Well, don't look at me. If a chicken won't do it, that's the bottom of my bag of tricks."

"Well, a chicken might."

A friendly waitress led us to a table right by one of the fountains. Cara Mae didn't take her hat off and neither did I. Cowboys didn't take their hats off inside, not for anything but church. And I liked being a cowboy — wearing my boots and hat, keeping my leather gloves stuffed in my back pocket, rolling up the sleeves of my two new shirts, both with a yoke in the back, both with snaps instead of buttons. I liked having the tourists in their bermudas and flowered shirts stare at us curiously. And I liked sitting with Cara Mae, looking like a couple — not just a couple of kids. It didn't seem possible that I'd ever sit in a classroom again, bareheaded and in running shoes.

"This is a cool place," Cara Mae said, looking around, "but can we really afford to eat here?"

"I just bet two hundred dollars. Twenty more isn't going to make that much difference."

"I'm not very hungry, anyway."

Behind us the mariachi band started up, and the folks from out of state smiled and kept time with their forks.

"I don't think they know 'La Cucaracha' means 'The Cockroach,' do you?"

She grinned at me and reached for my hand.

"Hey, there's my uncle," I said, waving the other one.

"Where?"

"Over there. The one getting up."

"And here I am in a T-shirt."

"So what. He's wearing a T-shirt, too." And jeans. Tight jeans. Very tight jeans.

"Pull up a chair," I said after I'd introduced him and Cara Mae.

"Just for a second. Billy tells me you know all there is about horses," he said to her.

"Not really," she replied, playing with her napkin.

"And that you can win that bet."

"Yes, sir. I hope so."

I could tell she was embarrassed, so I squeezed her hand encouragingly.

"That shirt," he said, "is the perfect color for your eyes."

Cara squirmed in her chair and looked pleased.

"I spotted you guys a few seconds ago, and I was just telling my friend Suzette how good you two looked together." He beamed at us. "And speaking of Suzette, I'd better get back there." He stood up. "Are you okay?" He said to me. "Need anything?"

"Just two hundred dollars. I'm a big tipper."

"Very funny." He pushed my hat down over my eyes. Then he said goodbye to Cara and shook her hand.

"Nice," she said when Wes was out of earshot.

"What'd you expect?"

"I don't know, that he'd be weird or something. Is that stupid?"

"Probably some gay guys are weird, but he's not."

"And cute. I love mustaches." She rolled her eyes. "That little butt and those broad shoulders . . ."

"I wish that ran in the family."

"Get serious. I think you're cute."

"Maybe, but it's all a lot closer to the ground."

We were almost finished eating when I saw Suzette get up and head for the bathroom, so I excused myself and went over to Wes's table.

"Hi, kiddo," he said. "She's a sweetheart."

I leaned toward him. "Are those your pants?" I hissed.

"Of course they're my pants. Why?"

"They're so tight."

"They're supposed to be tight."

I toyed with a broken tortilla chip. "When are you going to be home tonight?"

"Gosh, whenever you say, Dad. But can I have ten dollars for a condom after the movie?"

"What do you want a condom for?" I asked, loud enough so people eating beside us paused and looked over.

"I was just kidding. Relax. I'll be home when I get there."

"You aren't really going to the movies, are you?"

He put his bottle of Carta Blanca down deliberately.

"I'm going to drop Suzette off, then I'm going to the bars. Okay?"

"What bars?"

He glanced around conspiratorially, then whispered, "The *gay* bars."

"Are you going by yourself?"

"Why do I feel like a fifteen-year-old girl in her first miniskirt?"

"Okay, okay," I said, getting up. "Just be careful, that's all."

Cara Mae had found something she liked on the radio, and it was playing softly as I eased up the hill by her house.

"Anything wrong?" she asked. "You look like you've got something on your mind."

"I was just thinking about my uncle. He's going out tonight."

"With that lady from the restaurant?"

"Uh-uh. By himself. To the bars."

"He's over twenty-one," she said sensibly.

I didn't know what good it would do to get into the gay part, so I just said, "You seem a little thoughtful yourself."

"I am. I'm thinking about The Dark Mirage." She leaned my way and curled one hand inside my thigh. "And you. I'm thinking how I like you more and more all the time."

There went any worries about Wes, because I knew by the way she looked at me and touched me that we were going to make love. That's what made it so great. No wondering, none of those weird and embarrassing maneuvers.

"Billy," she whispered a few minutes later.

"What?" I said, unbuttoning her jeans.

"I'll bet she needs a run-out bit."

I stopped at the second button.

"The Dark Mirage. I'll bet she needs a different bit."

"Well, jeez, Cara."

"Sorry."

We started in again. I wasn't discouraged. What do hormones know. And she was soft and hard in all the right places.

Cara held her arms up like a referee signaling a touchdown and I slipped her T-shirt off. As it covered her eyes for a second she said, "I'll bet she needs blinkers, too."

"Well, sonofabitch." I dropped the shirt and it hung around her neck like a huge bandanna. "All I'm doing is thinking about you and all you're doing is thinking about that horse."

"You're jealous," she said, sounding amazed.

"I am not."

"You are too."

"I am too," I admitted.

Cara laughed and leaned into me. Her skin was so soft and smooth.

"Let's go see her," I said all of a sudden.

"Who?"

"The Dark Mirage."

"Really?"

"Sure."

She slipped back into her T-shirt. "Are you mad?"

"Nah, it's okay. Anyway, when you see us together, you'll realize that she may be taller, but I've got a cuter hat."

It was past midnight before I pulled into the driveway in Nuevo Grande. The garage was empty and the house was dark.

Well, I reasoned, so what? Cara's right. He's over twenty-one. If he wants to stay out till all hours and worry his relatives sick, he can.

"The hell with him," I said out loud as I brushed my teeth a few minutes later. "I'll just go to bed."

But I slept terribly. I was like a toy boat in a busy pond: every little wave rocked me. A coyote, someone's car, spooky house noises, a telephone somewhere down

159

the block. And all the time looking at the clock. I never wanted to hear the phrase "time flies" again. Oozes, maybe. Or slogs.

When I heard the van at two-thirty and the solid thunk of the front door, I got up, walked down the hall, and peeked into the dining room.

"What are you doing up?" Wes asked, pouring himself a drink.

"Uh, going to the bathroom."

"Not right there, I hope. That's a Navajo rug."

"Ha, ha." I started strolling toward the couch. "Are you okay?"

"Of course."

"Good. Great. Did you have fun?"

"If you call fun standing in a bar with a dozen other guys all dressed like the Hardy Boys."

"That's all you did, just stand there and then come home?"

"First I jerked off, Inspector."

"What? In the bar?"

"I went home with someone, Billy. Then I jerked off. That's what we do now," he said, losing his tolerance just a little. "We go to the bars like we used to, we play eyesie-looksie like we used to, we go home with somebody like we used to, but then we just masturbate."

"Each other?"

He shook his head. "No."

"And that's what safe sex is?"

"What'd you think it was, not getting broken glass in your kneecaps?"

"And that's what you did tonight?"

"And only that."

I sat down across from him, realized I was wearing only my shorts, jumped up, was ashamed of myself, sat down again.

"I forget sometimes," I said slowly, "that we're not just guys sharing an apartment and all that. Roommates. I forget we're different."

"Well, you're right. We are."

"Will you not get mad if I ask you something else?"

"Who knows."

"Do you kiss these guys?"

"Sometimes."

"Yuk."

"Do you kiss Cara Mae?"

"Well, sure."

"Yuk," he said.

"Okay. Okay. I get it, and I apologize. But I don't really understand all this." I ran my hands through my hair. "Did you even like this guy tonight? What was his name?"

"Alex."

"Did you like him?" I repeated.

"If I answer this correctly, do I get the luggage and the fabulous, fun-filled trip to old Mexico?"

"You did, didn't you?"

"Okay," he admitted. "I liked him. And I'm wondering if he'll call me." Then he grinned. "Satisfied, Sherlock?"

"Can I ask one more stupid question? Did you always know you were gay?"

"Absolutely. I just didn't know what to call it at first."

* * *

Next morning Lew and I had just finished putting away the last bag of Ranchmaster feed when Cara Mae rode up with a dog and a cat, or — to be exact — a puppy and a kitten. She dismounted by swinging one leg over the saddle horn, then sliding off: no hands.

"What's with the menagerie?" asked Lew.

"Where's your chicken, Billy?" she asked. "I want to try something."

"Is this the same chicken," said Lew, "that he chokes regularly, or another one?"

"What's up?" I asked, disregarding him and peering into the nearest stall, where Chicken Little was asleep.

"I'm hoping The Dark Mirage wants a pal like Moon's Medicine did."

"That'll calm her down?"

"Exactly." She thrust the puppy at Lew. "Hold him while I try the other one, okay?"

He retreated, both hands in the air like a person who is Not Involved.

"C'mon, now." Cara tugged at the gray kitten. With all twenty claws stuck in her T-shirt, it looked like a huge wad of chewing gum.

"Just toss 'em all in at once," I advised, "and let the filly pick who she likes."

Even Lew watched as the three of them roamed among the shiny hooves, sniffing the straw or rubbing up against her legs. The Dark Mirage scowled down like an evangelist.

"She won't play with them," Lew observed, "but she might eventually eat one."

"Shoot!" Cara sat down with a thump.

"Now what?"

"First take these animals back. Then I got one more idea. You guys wait here, okay?"

Lew and I settled down on a bench in the shade and watched her mount up.

"You know," he said a few second later, "she looks a lot better than she did two months ago." He leaned in. "What's it like, anyway?"

I stared at him. "You really think I'm about to tell you?"

"I'd tell you what it was like with Abby."

"I don't want to know what it's like with Abby."

"Really?"

"Well," I said after a pause, "not enough to tell you what it's like with Cara."

Lew shook his head. "That's what happens to a guy who holds furry little animals."

A couple of exercise girls strolled by in tight jeans and chaps, their tummies showing under the cut-off T-shirts. Lew groaned and took off his hat.

"Do you and Abby do it every time you're together?" I asked.

"If I tell you, will you tell me?"

"Sure."

"Yeah, we do."

"We don't."

He looked me up and down. "You're okay, aren't you? Everything works?"

"Of course everything works. But last night I guess she was thinking about other stuff."

"Other guys? Which one? We'll bust his head."

I pointed. "Other girls. Girl horses."

"Well, Abby and I were parked out in the boonies."

"Doing it. I know, I know."

"Not really.

"I thought you said . . ."

"I exaggerated a little. We just had a few beers and looked up at the stars." Lew took off his hat and ran his hand through his hair, which he'd tried to even out with the horse clippers. What was left was brown at the roots, still bleached white at the ends like the lawns in Bradleyville after the first frost.

"Abby was bummed about going away, you know, to the Coast. It wasn't too bad sitting there. I had a couple of deep thoughts."

"Like what?"

"Like wondering why she didn't feel like doing it."

"And the answer was?"

"I don't know. That *was* the thought, see: wondering why not."

"You said you had two. What was the other one?"

He leaned toward me. "You know that secret sauce they use on the barbecue beef in the backstretch cafeteria? I was wondering what's in it."

"Those were the deep thoughts?"

"Yeah," he said. "Not deep enough for you, Einstein?"

"No, they're fine. It's just that if you're thinking about being a philosopher I wouldn't quit my day job just yet."

"Fuck you," he said mildly.

I bumped him hard enough to almost knock him off the bench; he bumped me back. Then we just sat like that, shoulders barely touching, both of us grinning, until — a few minutes later — Cara came back.

Lew hopped up in a hurry. "What's that for?"

She plopped a melon down beside me. "Give me your knife, Lewie."

He dug into his fatigues and came up with a weapon bigger than a harmonica. We watched him try to open it.

"Handy," I commented.

"Well, it's got fifty blades," he explained, "one for every kind of aggressor."

"Find the one for the Invasion of the Watermelons."

"I got to stop biting my nails," he complained as Cara took the knife away from him, popped a blade out, and started to slice away.

"Now we all eat a little to show her how good it is."

"Is this masculine enough for you," I asked, "or do you want to smash it against your forehead?"

"Shut up," he said, trying not to laugh.

"Now," Cara Mae said, "we see if she eats it."

"What if she doesn't?"

"We start saving our money again."

"Speaking of money," said Lew, "there's the little matter of two hundred dollars."

"I've got it, don't worry."

Cara Mae swung the bottom of the stall door shut, laid a slice of melon on the ledge, and stepped back. Pretty soon The Dark Mirage stepped up, looking around warily, then snatched it.

"All right!" Cara Mae said.

"Now what?"

"Now we just feed her till she's used to us."

"She takes it right out of our hands," said Lew, "with those teeth?"

"Right. Then we get in the stall with her, then we put a saddle on and walk her, then I get up on her and we go five furlongs."

When I stepped up with another piece, back went the filly's ears. So I just laid it on the ledge. "Do we have enough time for all this to happen?" I asked.

Cara shrugged. "We'd better."

10

Cara Mae took a deep breath, let it out, and said, "We might as well get this workout over with."

"Is Jack out there already?" Lew asked.

"Uh-huh," she replied, glancing toward his office, "along with just about everybody else in the world, and all of 'em with stopwatches."

"Fletcher and Grif?" I asked.

"Count on it."

"Did that filly of theirs work earlier?"

"She went so-so," Cara Mae said uneasily. "But wait'll they get a load of this one."

We looked at The Dark Mirage rolling her eyes, starting to break out in a nervous lather up around her withers.

"She's already too hot," said Lew.

"It don't mean a thing," Cara assured us as she gingerly put one foot in the stirrup and slithered on like a horse thief.

"If she gets real nasty," Lew whispered to me, "get an ear in your mouth and bite hard. That'll calm her down."

"You get her ear in your mouth; thank God I'm too short for that."

We led her through the backstretch toward the gap in the railing where all the horses started their workouts. She didn't get any worse, but she was a handful, shying at the least little thing and sometimes just stopping dead like an old mule.

We started to pass more people all the time. It seemed half the backstretch was lined up like they were waiting for a parade.

"She don't look that bad," someone commented.

"If you're talkin' about the girl, you're right. Otherwise, I'm not so sure." Then they both laughed.

"My fifty," said another man, "says she'll come apart like a cheap Chinese suitcase."

"What's that filly's name, anyway, Bundle of Nerves?"

"Hey," I pleaded, "how about giving us a break, okay?"

"Bunch of goddamn sadists," said Lew, scowling.

As we passed the official clocker and told him the horse's name, Cara Mae asked us to walk her out onto the track before we turned loose of the halter.

"I'll be okay now," she said, adjusting her beat-up helmet. "Just let her stand awhile if she wants."

I patted her on the leg. "Be careful. If she gets crazy, just bail out."

Cara shook her head. "Not with Jack watching. If she goes down, I go down with her."

"You're an exercise girl, not a ship's captain."

Lew and I drifted back toward the other people. Abby came up and put her arm through his, so I just kept going, glancing over my shoulder every now and then to see how things were progressing. Cara Mae was still letting the filly stand and look things over. The Dark Mirage seemed awful nervous to me, glancing around like she was watching for the cops.

"Well," Jack said, "let's see how smart we are." He walked up beside me and shouted. "Anytime, Cara Mae."

She waved her whip and clucked. Nothing. Like sitting on a marble general's marble horse. Cara Mae rocked a little and dug with her heels.

Jack showed me his stopwatch. "Doesn't look like I'm gonna need this, does it," he said dryly.

"Wait. Look!"

The filly had taken off on her own, moving sideways, shaking her head and starting to fight Cara.

"Straighten her out, Sugar," Abby shouted.

It was like the horse heard and was determined to be contrary. She stopped dead in her tracks and — when Cara Mae was off balance — reared up like the handsome cowboy's stallion at the end of all those old Westerns. Except that Cara Mae had to grab a fistful of mane just to stay on.

"I'm givin' two-to-one," shouted Fletcher, "she don't beat my filly week after next, and ten-to-one right now she don't finish this workout at all."

The sound of thirty-five half-wit cowboys laughing is not the sweetest in the world. I was red in the face as I glanced over at Jack, who was studying the situation through his binoculars.

"I just wish," he muttered, "she'd run a little so I could . . . whoops!"

The two of them were about halfway down the backstretch, with The Dark Mirage rearing and propping and dancing sideways, when all of a sudden she just took the bit between her teeth and went.

Cara Mae was caught off guard for a second or two, and then there was nothing to do but try to get the filly to stop. As they rounded the turn, Cara was back in the stirrups, pulling with all her might. One of the outriders — a guy with a fast quarterhorse who worked for the track — took off after her but didn't get hold until they were past the wire and almost through the clubhouse turn.

He led Cara back. As she passed, there was all this sarcastic applause from the people who'd bet on French Bred.

"First part of that," somebody shouted, "was a little slow, but you sure made up for it in the last three-eighths."

"I almost had her," Cara Mae fumed to the outrider as they got up to us. "I could have handled it myself. I could have."

"Here you go, Jack," said the outrider.

Jack looked up at Cara, who was pale as the moon. "You okay?"

"I almost had her. She wasn't running away."

"Uh-huh," said Jack, squatting down to feel the horse's fetlocks.

Abby held The Dark Mirage while Lew and I gave her a bath and watered her down. Cara Mae sat on the bench at the end of the long shed and smoked.

"I don't imagine," said Lew, "that she's in the mood to be playfully squirted with a hose."

"I don't imagine," I agreed.

"See if she wants to eat with us," Abby suggested.

I watched Cara Mae light another cigarette with the one she was already smoking.

"Okay," I said dubiously.

As I walked away, the filly shied and Abby jerked hard on the shank. I made a wide turn away from those back hooves and sidled up beside my girlfriend. I decided to try the light touch.

"If every one of those things takes an hour off your life, maybe you'll be lucky and just skip next Monday."

She looked down at the cigarette. "They're my lungs."

"I was just kidding."

She took a big breath and let it out. "Yeah, sorry." She ground the filter into a bucket of sand. "These things taste like somebody's shorts, anyway."

I reached down and put my hand on her shoulder, just lightly, no big deal. Still, I felt her shake a little, and when she looked up at me her eyes were wet.

"Why can't I do anything right?" she asked, her voice breaking.

"You didn't do anything wrong."

"I couldn't hold her," she said.

"Nobody could've."

"I was so glad to see that outrider. I thought my arms were gonna fall off."

"Nothing happened, though. Nobody got hurt and she didn't run off and break a leg."

"I should've been able to, though. I told Jack I could.

I told you guys." She waved to include Lew and Abby, who'd drifted over.

"You'll do better next time, Hon," Abby said.

Cara Mae snorted. "If there is a next time. What's Jack gonna think?"

"He didn't say you couldn't ride her, did he?" I pointed out. "And anyhow, I heard him say he'd bet on the race himself."

Cara Mae threw up her hands. "Oh, great. Now I've got to worry about his money, too."

"Oh, forget the money, Sugar," said Abby.

"You forget it," she snapped. "Money don't mean nothing to you, but it's Billy's money for college and my money so I don't look like some racetrack tramp at Phoenix High."

"She just meant," I pointed out, "that the bet's made, and worrying and blaming yourself won't help."

"Right," said Abby gratefully. "That's what I meant."

Cara nodded, wagged her head helplessly, sighed again. "I'm just sorry I got you guys into this, that's all."

"We got ourselves into it," said Lew. "Billy and me."

"Right. I could've told Lew to cool it, or I could've told those guys we didn't want to bet, but I didn't. And that was before you'd even seen the horse."

"But I'm the one said she was better than French Bred. I'm the one said four or five weeks was all she'd need. If she loses on Labor Day, it's all my fault."

"No, it's not," I insisted. "Nothing's all anybody's fault."

"C'mon," said Abby, putting her arm around Cara's shoulders, "let's get some tacos and forget all this for a little while."

172

But Cara Mae jerked herself away as Abby looked at me and raised her eyebrows in what amounted to a shrug.

"C'mon," I said softly. "I don't want to go if you don't."

"I'd just be such piss-poor company, Billy."

"You guys go on," I said to the others, "I'll just . . ."

Cara Mae didn't say a word, but all of a sudden she just took off running. I called after her, but she didn't turn around.

Abby put her hand on my arm. "Let her go, Billy. She'll be okay."

"I haven't seen anybody do that in years," said Wes, helping himself to more salad.

"What?"

"Make a little lake with his mashed potatoes and then drop peas in."

"I had a late lunch and I'm feeling a little weird. Maybe I'll drive down to the U. of A. Want to go?"

He shook his head. "Can't. My night on the AIDS hotline. What's down there?"

"The other day I saw something on the bulletin board in the paymaster's office about a major in racetrack management." I moved my piece of fish around again, making it swim toward Gravy Lake.

"Is that what's got you worried tonight — the future?"

"Cara Mae, too. She had a bad day."

Wes put his fork down and shook his head. "You're so much like your dad. In college he could never just sleep with somebody. He'd always worry about them, too."

"Did my dad sleep with a lot of girls?"

"Any woman above the age of eighteen who had long, straight hair and knew the words to 'Michael, Row the Boat Ashore.'"

"You're kidding."

"He didn't tell you?"

"It never came up at the dinner table."

"How about when real men get together in their flannel shirts to swap stories?"

I shook my head.

"Well, he had a big rep at one time."

"But Mom doesn't have long, straight hair."

"To her undying credit."

I put my fork down. "I think I miss my folks a little tonight."

"Well, it won't be long now."

"Yeah, but then I'll miss Tucson and you."

"And Cara."

"Uh-huh."

"Want a little advice?"

"Eat my dinner because there are children in India who are too fat already?"

"Very funny, but no. Why don't you just drive down to the university?"

I got to my feet. "Okay. But I'll help you clean up first."

"I can get it."

"I know, but I want to."

Coasting down from the foothills later that evening, I thought how funny it felt being alone. I was used to having Cara Mae beside me. I wondered if she was getting high, and I pictured her coming around the next morning saying, "I'm sorry," like she always did.

The campus was almost deserted. Tall, wavy palms stood on each side of the curving road that led from Park Avenue onto the university itself, and each palm had a light of its own like a statue or a Hollywood star.

The building with the racetrack management offices was open, so I picked up a handful of brochures, then wandered back out into the well-lit night. There was a deli on University Avenue, just past Campus Drugs with its year-round display of Coppertone and Ray Bans. I went in, got an iced tea from a girl in a Tri-Delt tank top, and sat at a table by the window.

Naturally, racetrack management was a lot more complicated than I'd imagined: immigration problems, unions, insurance, fan psychology, and taxes. The list of classes went on and on.

I was staring out the window trying to see the future when two girls walked past, stopped, and smiled. They stood there a second, egging each other on, laughing and goofing around. Then one of them tapped herself on the head.

"What?" I asked silently, raising both hands to show I couldn't hear.

She tapped again and mouthed, "Take off your hat."

So I did.

They whispered, nodded, giggled, then gave me the thumbs-up and a couple more big smiles before they darted away.

For once I didn't blush. It didn't mean anything, anyway, and I liked my curly hair, which had gotten longer that summer. I was flattered, but not enough to go running after them. I wondered, though, if they'd care that I was short. Well, what if they did? That was their tough luck. I didn't. For once in my life, I didn't.

"So did you just go home then?" asked Lew as he closed the door to The Dark Mirage's stall. "You didn't find out their names?"

"Uh-uh." I cut up the last of some melon. "I wandered around the house until Wes came home. I didn't even read."

"Who reads?"

"I don't know. Lately, it's like my own life is more interesting than the ones in books."

"Hold it. Here comes the heroine of this story."

Cara Mae rode up slowly, giving a little nod when Lew said hi as he passed. As usual, I leaned against her leg and talked up to her.

"You okay?"

"I feel like shit," she said, drooping.

"Is that why the sunglasses?"

She nodded. "You don't want to see my eyes."

"What happened?"

"Oh, I smoked a lot of dope, then got into my daddy's beer. Ended up barfing on a little barrel cactus out back."

I patted her leg consolingly.

"I was just so mad at myself." She moved a little in the saddle, but only a little and like all her bones hurt. "That is so dumb," she said slowly, "to hurt myself more when I'm already hurting. And I've done it just about my whole life."

"I've never seen you like this before," I said.

"It's been better this summer. Or I have." She took one hand off the reins and touched my hat. I rested my chin on her knee.

"Let me get you some aspirin."

"I'm okay."

"No, you're not. And, anyway, I want to."

11

I don't want to give the impression that there was nothing else going on at the track except the race between The Dark Mirage and French Bred. Besides the regular menu of nine races a night three nights a week, what people were really talking about was the Tucson Derby, with a hundred-thousand-dollar purse and all the good horses that were shipping in from all over to try and get a piece of it.

We were running against Fletcher's filly earlier that night — in the fourth race, to be exact — so the summer would end for us two hours earlier than for most people.

Well, to be fair, even on August twenty-first, the day The Dark Mirage was scheduled to have her second workout, the summer was over for some people. Without enough money coming in to even pay for stall space and feed, they'd pulled out early with their handful of sore horses. So the backstretch had this funny feeling to it: intense in a way and in another way running down like an old clock. And when Lew and I led The Dark Mirage onto the track for the workout, there weren't as many people watching. Maybe the novelty had worn off; maybe they had chores of their own to do.

"Maybe," said Lew, looking around, "they already decided they can't lose."

"She's not near so nervous," said Cara Mae, tucking the whip in her back pocket.

"I think I'll eat some watermelon if that's what it does for you," I said. "I'm starting to dream about this race."

Jack waved and walked over to meet us. "How's she feel?" he asked.

"A little on the muscle," said Cara Mae.

"Let's try and get five furlongs today. Use her a little if you can, get her tired." He nodded at the nearest striped pole, each one marking an eighth of a mile. "And turning for home, pop her a couple of times and show her the stick. If she don't want it, then Pedroza rides without one, okay?"

Cara nodded, Lew and I let go of the halter, and she was on her own. Up the homestretch a ways, a big, rough-looking stallion threw her rider, then just stood there while the girl got up, holding her elbow and swearing.

"Sometimes I don't know how I ever did it," said Jack softly.

"Did what?" I asked.

"Got up on some sore-legged thing that didn't want to be rode anyway, and went about forty miles an hour right alongside eight or nine other peckerheads too dumb or too little to do anything else." He raised his binoculars. "Now why isn't that filly even trying?"

The Dark Mirage was running, but even I could see she wasn't putting out. As they turned for home, Cara Mae showed her the whip and whacked her a time or two. But right-handed she shied left, and left-handed she shied right.

"Well," Jack said, "at least we know that."

The three of us walked up to meet Cara Mae, who was jogging back near the rail.

"You're the rider," Jack said. "You tell me."

"It's down there, but she won't use it."

"She's not hurtin'?"

Cara shook her head. "No, but everything spooks her: birds, shadows, piece of paper on the track. And especially the starting gate."

"If there was some way to get her off by herself," I said. "Maybe she'd relax."

"Yeah," Lew sneered. "Send her on a cruise with a couple hundred watermelons."

"Wait a minute," said Jack. "Billy might have something." He frowned and scratched his hat for a few seconds before he asked, "How'd all of you like to work about twice as hard for the next ten days, not get paid any more, but maybe win that bet?"

Lew, Cara, and I looked at one another. "What's up?" I asked.

"I'll call Charlie Wright at Tanque Verde," Jack said thoughtfully. "And Lew, you'll have to hold up your end around here and maybe Billy's too, all right?"

"I'm in."

"Hold it, hold it," I said. "What's Tanque Verde?"

"Little training center that never caught on. But there's a starting gate and the track's in pretty good shape."

"You think Billy's right, don't you?" asked Cara. "That she can be by herself out there and maybe settle down."

Jack grinned at her. "Tomorrow or the next day you and Billy take the old Chevy pickup and van her on out there. Charlie'll be expecting you."

As long as I didn't think about going back to Bradley-ville, things were fine. For example, when Cara and I took the horses out to Tanque Verde a couple of days later, she sat right beside me. We talked the whole way about the race and about The Dark Mirage: what Jack had said about working her and when, how she'd take to the new place, what a difference we hoped it'd make.

At Sabino Canyon Road a new Buick oozed up beside the old truck we were driving. In the back, sitting next to his sister, probably, was a kid about my own age. He was just staring up at me, at us. I smiled back and touched my hat brim with one finger. He raised his hand and waved, wiggling three of his fingers.

That felt so great. *I* felt great, because I was sure I knew what he was thinking: *Look at that cowboy and his girlfriend.* And it was true. I was a cowboy and I did have a girlfriend. I was somebody with something.

The Tanque Verde training center wasn't much more than thirty or forty stalls and a half-mile training track tucked back among some giant rocks at the end of a long box canyon.

Jack's friend Charlie turned out to be a man about my dad's age. He helped us unload the horses and the tack once we'd all shaken hands and said hello.

It was past four when we finished, and Cara said she

was thinking about saddling up and galloping The Dark Mirage.

"Just to get her used to the place," she said. "Think it's too hot?"

Charlie looked at the shadows on the boulders. "Half an hour wouldn't hurt, I don't think." He shifted a wad of chewing tobacco and looked over at me. "Billy?"

"What's that in your mouth?" Cara Mae asked a few minutes later.

"Muffing."

"A muffin?"

I shifted the glob. "Nothing."

She looked down at me skeptically.

"Okay, okay. It's tobacco."

"Chewing tobacco?"

"In name only. I'm not chewing *this* stuff."

"Then why . . . ?"

"Charlie gave it to me. I didn't want him to think . . . you know."

"Just spit it out, Billy."

I moved it around some more so I could talk. It was tricky stuff. "What, and ruin the environment?"

"Well, I'm not kissing you until you do."

I stepped behind the filly to spit, but I couldn't do that right, either. It exploded in little wet flakes. "How do they manage that in the movies?" I asked. "It goes right in the spittoon. I'd need a net."

Cara Mae angled out of the saddle and wiped my mouth with the back of her glove. "Now give me a kiss," she said, "and let me work this horse."

I glanced over my shoulder. "Can you lean down some more? Charlie's watching and I don't want to have to get up on my tiptoes."

Cara glanced at him, then me. "I used to think it was easy being a guy," she said. Then she leaned down the way trick riders do when they're going to snatch a handkerchief off the ground, put her arm around my neck, and kissed me passionately. "Tell him," she whispered, "that I just can't keep my hands off you."

The sides of the canyon weren't all that high, but the way the rocks were, shadows fell across the track even at four-thirty. Cara and The Dark Mirage moved in and out of the blazing light. She was riding without a helmet and her blond hair was truly like gold.

"Can she beat that French Bred?" Charlie asked, joining me at the rail.

"Even Jack's not sure," I said, hedging.

"Fletcher and Grif know you're out here," he said calmly.

I'd been draped across the weathered timber, but that brought me to attention. "They do?"

Charlie nodded. "Some peckerwood called up and asked for Jack."

"What'd you say?"

"That I'd never heard of him, but that don't mean nothin'. There's no secrets around a racetrack, son. That's why Fletcher's worried. His filly's not gettin' any better and yours is."

"Nothing he can do about that," I said, feeling cocky.

"Don't be too sure." Charlie aimed, spit at a lizard,

and missed. "Him and Grif stand to lose four or five thousand dollars if their horse don't win next weekend."

"I didn't know it was that much."

"They boarded a few head out here last year, then wouldn't pay me. So I get on my high horse and go into town, find 'em in the Panda Bar on Fourth Avenue, and call 'em out. I'd had a couple and they were gonna pay or else." He shook his head slowly. "Well, that Grif gets ahold of my throat and I start thinkin', this ain't worth three hundred dollars. I'm not proud of it, but I turned tail and run."

"You don't think he'd do anything to the horse, do you?"

"I'll put one of my boys close to her at night; then when you get back home I wouldn't let her out of my sight one minute the last forty-eight hours."

12

"This place is a mess," said Abby, looking around at the shabby barns of Tanque Verde.

"I guess you get used to it when you're here every day," I replied.

"Is this worth it?" asked Lew.

"She's not as jumpy as she was, but she's still not burning up the track. And today's the last workout. We run on Monday, if you can believe that."

"Daddy's sorry now he bet on that other horse," said Abby. "The news just ain't that good. Fletcher works her and it's the same thing every time."

"Maybe it's the same," I pointed out, "but it's not that bad."

She looked toward the racetrack, less than one-third the size of Sundown Park. "So you don't think he ought to make some side bets on our horse?"

"Abby, if I knew that, I'd bet more myself."

She let out a little hiss of exasperation. "Well, I am goin' to the bathroom."

Lew and I watched her walk away in a mini-huff.

"How is she, really?" Lew asked slyly. "You can tell me."

"Like I said — calmer than she used to be, but not much faster."

"Damn it," he said. "Then we could lose."

Across the way, Cara was jogging The Dark Mirage. As I watched, they broke into an easy gallop.

"What the hell's wrong with that horse, anyway?" Lew demanded.

"Nothing," I murmured, still watching Cara Mae.

"What?"

"Nothing," I yelled. "Look at that."

The filly was running. Cara Mae had her face right down in the mane. She was dead still in the stirrups, her legs taking all the shock, her back so straight you could've balanced a plate on it.

"Wow," said Abby, appearing in time to clutch Lew's arm. "Look at her go."

They swept around the turn. The filly had her ears pricked. She was all business, and when they hit the wire, Cara straightened up and waved her whip to the invisible, admiring crowd.

The three of us clapped when she jogged up, slid to the ground, and took off her helmet and gloves. "If she'll do that Saturday night we're home free," she said with a grin.

"You looked great, kid," said Abby.

"I didn't do anything," Cara Mae replied shyly. "It was her."

"Now," said Lew, taking charge, "we've got to keep her safe and sound, so we have to stand guard."

"All day?" Cara Mae asked.

"All day and all night. Especially all night. The only question is, who pulls which shift?"

"No way my dad's gonna let me stay out all night," Cara said, fiddling with her gloves.

"And I'm not sleeping on a cot in some stinky tack room, either," added Abby.

"Then you two handle things in the daytime. They aren't going to try anything then, anyway. Billy and I'll take care of the rest."

"How?" I asked, picturing myself cowering in the dark barn alone while Grif's shadow — big as a boxcar — slid along the wall.

"We'll take turns sleeping."

"You'll be there, too?"

"Sure."

I breathed a quiet sigh of relief. "Okay."

Abby looked at her watch. "You vanning her back today?"

I nodded.

"Then I'll start in the morning and Cara can take the afternoons, okay?"

We turned to wave as Abby and Lew drove away, then I took the halter off the filly as Cara Mae fussed with the light saddle that race riders use.

"You looked terrific today," I said.

"Thanks."

I turned to hang the bridle on a peg. She still had her back to me, tugging at the cinch.

"You should think about being a real jockey. Just exercising horses isn't nearly good enough for you."

I watched her shoulders rise and fall. I saw her slump until her forehead pressed against the horse's heaving side.

"What am I going to do," she whispered, "without you around to tell me things like that?"

I walked up and put my arms around her. "C'mon," I said helplessly.

I stood on tiptoe and kissed her neck. Cara stepped back, right into me. I moved against her. One hand came up and grabbed my wrist hard. Then she turned around, breathing ragged. "Let's do it," she gasped. "Let's just do it."

"Okay. Sure." We kissed hard enough to bruise each other. "Here?"

"Anywhere. Up on the hill. I don't care."

Behind her The Dark Mirage shuddered and stamped.

"What about this horse?" I asked between kisses.

"What about her?"

"She's got to be washed."

"Well, let's wash her fast."

When I got home, the whole goddamn driveway was full of cars. I groaned out loud, remembering Wes's AIDS hotline fund-raiser.

Inside, I had to plow through some artsy types, all in silver and turquoise, all saying "Fabulous," all with pink drinks in fancy plastic glasses.

"And who is this macho morsel?" oozed someone with one pearl earring and a shirt with puffy buccaneer's sleeves.

"I live here," I muttered as I passed, but he took a wide step and blocked my way.

"This isn't an outfit, is it?" he asked, stroking my denim sleeve. "You've been — pardon the expression — working."

"Look, all I want to do is go to bed, okay?"

"I'm yours," he cried, clutching my arm and hamming it up for his friends.

"Stop handling me, man. I mean it!" I did, too, but he didn't exactly seem scared to death.

"I love it when they're stern," he breathed.

One of his pals pulled him away before I could take a swing. Then I lurked in the far corner of the living room while Wes cleared the house, herding people toward the front door, cutting one off as he bolted for the bar, holding up another who threatened to collapse on the sofa. Then he kissed Suzette on the cheek, closed the door, and leaned on it.

"Whew. I suppose it was worth it, but what an ordeal."

"Who was that weenie in the Captain Hook shirt?" I asked grumpily.

"Mickey Thompson?"

"Well, he was screwing around or coming on to me or something. It gave me the creeps."

"Sounds like Mickey. He can be a little predatory."

"I guess I thought all gay guys were like you."

"Which I'll take as a compliment." He leaned over the coffee table and started to pick up glasses and ashtrays.

"Sex is stupid, anyway," I said.

He looked at me for a second. "You sound tired, kiddo. Why not get some sleep."

"Okay." But I just stood there. "I'll help you clean up first."

"You don't have to."

"I couldn't sleep anyway."

We worked for a minute or two. Then I dropped something.

"Shit," I said, kicking the plastic glass across the room.

"What happened between you and Cara Mae?" Wes asked, sitting down and patting the cushion beside him.

"We had a fight."

"Why don't you take your hat off," he said, picking up his drink. "I feel like you're about to rush out of here and head off a stampede."

I told him the whole sordid story. "Then she told me to go to hell and I came on home."

As Wes took a big swallow of Wild Turkey, I peered into my hat. Even that looked stupid. It wouldn't hold ten gallons. It wouldn't even hold a quart. I was a pint-sized person wearing a pint-sized hat.

"When you tell Cara you love her," Wes asked, stroking his mustache thoughtfully, "what does she say?"

I jiggled my tiny hat. "I don't know. I never told her."

"But you do love her."

"I think so."

"Have you told her that?"

"That I *think* I love her?"

"Why not? It's honest."

"If it's honesty you want, I honestly wanted her more tonight than I ever have. That's what's so confusing. One minute we're out at Tanque Verde just talking and the next we're all over each other."

"Sounds okay to me."

"It was, and then we decide to go back up to the hill

where we always park. So I'm driving about a thousand miles an hour and we're kissing at stoplights but then we get up there and . . . I don't know. I didn't want to anymore, or I couldn't or something."

"Ever hear of the wisdom of the penis?" he asked.

"The what?"

"It just means that if you won't talk about it, your pecker will."

I looked at him doubtfully and then at my pants, like I actually expected it to say something.

"You're not impotent, if that's what your worried about."

"Tell that to Cara."

"It'll be obvious. And then afterward you can tell her how you're feeling. How you're *really* feeling."

"Why should I talk to her? She told me to go to hell."

"She cares enough to get mad at you. If you really like somebody, it means you can really dislike him, too. Feelings are like coins: they don't come with just one side."

"She does like me, doesn't she?" I asked quietly.

"Of course she does."

"I'm so afraid of losing her," I said suddenly, "and of never seeing her again." Immediately I was all choked up, so I picked up my hat and hid my face in it. "I don't want you to see me cry." My voice sounded funny and hollow.

"I don't mind," he said, leaning toward me and tugging at the hat.

"I look ugly," I said, really starting to bawl.

"I've seen worse."

About a minute later I pulled away. "Jeez," I gasped. "I got snot on your shirt."

"That's what dry cleaners are for. And when they ask me what it is I'll say, 'Snot, thank you. My nephew was having a hard time and he wasn't afraid to act like it.' Then they'll give me the Good Uncle discount."

I laughed a little — a nervous half-laugh–half-sob — and wiped my nose on my sleeve. "What do I do now, apologize to Cara?"

"More or less. Just talk to her. Tell her the truth."

"Okay." Then I fell back into the couch. "Boy, what an ordeal. And now I'm supposed to say to her, 'I love you and I'm leaving you'? If I love her, shouldn't I want to stay with her forever?"

Wes shrugged. "There's all kinds of love," he said.

"I'll bet she thinks I should stay."

"Ask her," he said simply.

13

Next morning Abby hung around The Dark Mirage while Lew and I worked. The backstretch was weirder than usual, and to give credit where it's due, Abby did a good job of guarding the horse, shooing away curious strangers. Once she called for Lew and me to come and take care of some stubborn cowboy who turned out to be a lot more interested in her than in anything with four legs.

All morning more people left for Phoenix or God knows where, nursing their old pickups another few hundred miles, hauling horse vans piled high with everything they owned. And all morning others — but not nearly as many — slid in, pulling candy-apple-red trailers with white pinstripes.

"They can't all be horses for the Derby, can they?" I asked Jack.

He nodded. "The purses are pretty good closing day, so they figure it's worth a trip."

Closing day. It seemed impossible. Forty-eight hours and the track would turn out its powerful lights and lock the big gates to the parking lot. The day after the day after that, I'd be home. *Home*. Another word that seemed hard to get hold of.

"I saw a maiden filly the other day," Jack said, "that looks like a winner if I ever saw one."

"Is she in our race on Saturday?"

"Uh-huh."

"The Dark Mirage can't beat her?"

Jack shrugged. "She came in from the Coast."

"If she's so hot, why ship her to a little track like this?"

Jack grinned at me. "Now you're thinking like a trainer," he said, turning away. "Oh, by the way, do you boys need a gun?"

"A gun? What for?"

"For tonight."

I pictured Lew and me shooting it out with Fletcher and Grif, sprinting from watering trough to barn like Butch Cassidy and the Sundance Kid.

"Are they going to have guns?"

"More than likely nothin' but a syringe full of Serpasil."

"What's that?"

"Tranquilizer."

"Maybe Lew and I should have one, too. That way the worst that could happen is we put each other to sleep."

"It's for the horse, Billy."

"Oh."

As Jack walked away shaking his head, Abby drifted over. She looked grouchy, and she was.

"Cara's *supposed* to be here," she said.

"Look, I want to talk to her about something anyway; I'll hang around and you can go home."

"Praise the Lord. I'm gettin' highlighted at two o'clock."

194

When I looked puzzled, she pointed to her hair.

"When she does come," Abby yelled, climbing into the pickup, "tell her I've got a bone to pick with her. I don't like for anybody to keep me waitin'."

"She'll be here any minute."

That was one-thirty.

"What are you doing here?" Lew asked, walking up with a cot under each arm. "I thought this was Cara's shift."

"I've been waiting all afternoon."

"Well, where the hell is she?"

"We had a fight."

"No shit. What about?"

I looked toward the parking lot. "Any more stuff in the truck?"

"You don't want to talk about it. Okay, there's lots more stuff in the truck."

We carried in just about everything Coleman made.

"Lew, we're going to be here two nights, not two years."

"You don't want cold beer?" he asked, plugging in a small refrigerator.

Finally we rigged a couple of lights and called it quits. I unrolled the blanket Wes had given me. It was pale blue cashmere and looked about as out of place as I felt.

"Help me finish up, okay?" Lew asked. "Before it gets dark."

Outside The Dark Mirage's stall we strung a small web of tripwires and gravel-filled tin cans to make an alarm system.

"Now, what happens when we hear something?" I asked, standing up to look things over.

"We take care of 'em."

"Yeah, but how?"

"I've got my knife," he said dubiously.

"And you should be able to get it open by October."

"I don't want to stab anybody, anyway." He thought for a second, running his hand over his bushy hair. "What if I just get in their way while you run for help."

"Is that what Rambo would do?"

"Screw him. He talks through his nose."

"Just kidding. It's a good plan. I can get to the guard's shack in about two minutes. They can't do much in two minutes, can they?"

"If they do, I'll just start screaming." He looked around at the deserted barns. "I sure wish we were up closer to the big outfits. Everybody around here has hauled ass."

"Jack's just staying for us, isn't he?" I asked.

"Pretty much. He put all the other horses in the big van this morning."

We looked toward The Dark Mirage next door.

"I hope she can beat that horse of Fletcher's," I said.

"Man, me too."

There's this time in the desert when it's not day anymore but not night, either. We could see the dark coming on as the part of the earth we were on turned away from the sun.

"What was that?" Lew whispered, and we both looked around.

"Jesus, I don't know. Should I turn on the light?"

"No. Wait. Yes."

"That about covers the possibilities."

"Shhhh." Lew slithered out of his cot and peered around the edge of the door.

"I don't see anything," he hissed.

"I think it was on the roof."

"Well, we know it's not Grif. He'd fall through."

The picture of the big moron tumbling down on top of us was too much, so we started to laugh. That scared the squirrel that'd scared us, so we didn't hear any more mysterious sounds.

We settled down and started to read. Lew had some back issues of *Soldier of Fortune*, and he flipped the pages lackadaisically. I read *Running in the Family*, remembering that I hadn't opened a book the whole summer. *Where was Cara and what was she doing?*

Just then the rocks in the can started to rattle. Lew shot off the cot and landed in the doorway. His fingers were arched into claws and he was screaming. Next door the horse kicked the walls.

"What is it?" I shouted once Lew had run out of air.

He leaped out into the passageway, screaming again. "Lew?" I yelled. "Lew, what is it?"

He peeked back in. "The chicken," he said breathlessly. "Caught in the strings."

"This is not going to work," I said as I cut Chicken Little free. "If it's not her, some dog or cat's going to stumble into it. Anyway, the horse will tell us if anybody tries anything."

"You're right," he said, kicking at the strings with his boot. "Forget it. We'll just take two-hour watches and

197

listen for the filly to act up. You start, okay? Go until ten, then wake me up and I'll go to midnight."

"Fine."

"Don't fall asleep," he said sternly. "This is no joke."

"Okay."

"I mean it, kid."

"I said okay!"

Staying awake was no problem. I had a few things on my mind, anyway. Or one thing. Or one person. When I did get a little sleepy, I walked next door and looked in on The Dark Mirage.

At ten sharp I shook Lew awake.

It was ten-twenty when something woke me, a horrible, guttural snarl like a maniac with a chainsaw. Panting, I sat up. There was Lew, crashed headfirst into his cot, snoring.

"Who could sleep," I said next morning, "with that going on." And I pointed to his nose.

"So I made it easy for you to stay awake."

"During *your* shift?"

"At least somebody was awake."

"How'd it go, boys?" said Jack, stopping by.

"No problem," Lew answered cheerily.

"Good. One more night and we're home free."

"One more night like this," I said, "and I'll sleep through the race on Monday."

"Go on home," Jack advised. "There's nothin' to do around here but keep an eye on one filly, and that's been taken care of. I wouldn't be here myself if it wasn't such a goddamn habit."

"He's right, Billy," said Lew. "I'll keep Abby company for a while and then I'll see you tonight."

"Look, when Cara shows, call me."

"I'll probably wake you up."

"I want you to. Don't forget!"

"Okay, okay. See you tonight."

I walked toward the van, then turned and asked, "You'll be here, won't you?"

Lew looked at me like I was crazy. "Tonight? Sure, I'll be here. It's my birthday. I always celebrate my birthday in a stall."

"Is it really your birthday?"

"Absolutely."

"Wow, nineteen."

"Eighteen, actually."

"You told me when I met you in June that you were eighteen."

He shrugged and grinned. "I lied."

"I thought you were Lew," said Abby when I pulled up to the stable that afternoon. "What the hell's goin' on here?"

"Where's Cara?" I asked, rubbing the sleep out of my eyes.

"Well, who knows where Cara is, and who cares."

"She didn't show up again?"

"Would I be here if she did?"

I looked north, as if I could see across the freeway and the desert all the way to Shadow Road. "Maybe I ought to drive out there."

Abby shook her head decisively. "No way, José. In

ten minutes this hot little body is gonna be soakin' in Jean Naté. You're on your own."

"Okay, okay. Lew'll be here at six and I'll go then."

When seven-thirty rolled around and Lew still wasn't there, the crackles got louder and the shadows got longer and scarier. Where in the hell was he? Did Fletcher and Grif have him? Would my turn come in an hour? Was all this part of some complicated plan? Would I die without telling Cara that I loved her?

"Take it easy," I said to myself. "You've seen too many movies."

I did this trick my mom'd taught me: I lay down and took ten deep breaths. Then I sprinted down to Jack's office, unlocked the door, and called Lew's house. Five rings later his mother answered. I casually asked for Lew.

"Is this Billy?" she asked.

I could hear the stereo in the background blaring "Proud Mary," a song I'd heard my folks play. "Yes, ma'am."

"Lew's been kidnapped, Honey. For his birthday."

"What?"

"Edgar ambushed him coming out of the bathroom right after lunch and I drove them both down to Sonoita and dropped them off."

"What?!" I was almost screaming. "What kind of present is that?"

"Oh," she said, sounding like this was going to explain things, "that's rattlesnake country."

"What in the world is that supposed to mean?"

"Lew likes a challenge," she answered, like I was the loony one.

"When's he coming back?"

"Tomorrow sometime. You can't move too fast through rattlesnake country at night, you know."

I was about to be the rudest I've ever been to a grown-up when I thought, What good will it do? "Thanks, Mrs. Coley," I said instead. Then I hung up and scurried back to my cot.

I'd just lain down when I heard a noise. A real one. Then another. Two real noises in a row: footsteps. I clutched my book like a real man. Then a shadow, thrown by the arc light behind the barn, grew on the opposite wall. And grew. And grew. Grif!

I slipped out of bed and stood in the dark. The only thing I couldn't figure out was why the filly wasn't acting up. Had he shot the tranquilizer into her like an arrow? Knocked her out with one punch? Turned her to stone just by looking at her?

I was determined to go down fighting. The minute he stepped into the doorway, I'd launch myself at him.

More footsteps. I wound myself tighter. They were getting closer.

"Billy?" someone whispered.

A battered hat peeked around the door. I'd seen that trick in the movies. How dumb did he think I was? I threw my book at it.

"Hey, what's the big idea?"

"Jesus! Cara, is that you?"

"Hi," she said sheepishly.

"Where in the world have you been?"

"Up on the hill. Most of the time. I even thought about

201

getting loaded. Three months ago I would've. But then I thought that's a hell of a way to treat someone you think a lot of. So I decided to come down and apologize."

"You don't have to do that. I'm the one who should be sorry."

"No, let me finish. I'm sorry I told you to go to hell. But I didn't know what was going on the other night. I still don't know. And maybe that's why I'm down here, not just to say I'm sorry but to find out." She looked me right in the eye. "Are you tired of me?"

"Oh, God, Cara. No. I was just so scared that I couldn't do it."

"What were you scared of?"

"Of telling you that I loved you and then getting on the train."

She looked around here, but the cots and lanterns and gear and even the refrigerator didn't seem to register.

"If you'd just said that, I wouldn't have told you to go to hell."

"I guess I'm saying it now."

Cara was wearing the gloves she rode in, even though I knew she'd driven the pickup. Methodically, she took them off.

"Well, then. Tell me."

I took a step closer. "I love you and I'm leaving day after tomorrow and I don't understand any of this."

"Well, I love you, too. And me neither."

I couldn't wait any longer. "I'm so glad to see you."

"God, Billy. Me too."

We'd just put our arms around each other and our hats had just collided the way they always did when we tried to kiss too fast when The Dark Mirage stirred next door.

"Shoot," Cara said. "Why does Lew have to show up now."

"Shhhh."

"What?"

"It's not Lew."

I reached up and turned out the light. We could hear the filly thrash around as she got to her feet. The sounds, lots of them, worked their way along the back wall, and we followed them with our eyes.

"What's going on?" Cara Mae whispered.

"It's Fletcher and Grif."

"Are you sure?"

"Who else?"

"What now?"

"Now we scream, I think."

"Just tell me when."

Beside us The Dark Mirage snorted and kicked.

"I'm going out there," I said finally.

"By yourself?"

"I could always take my book."

"I'll go, too."

A thousand things went through my mind at once, mostly brave little scenes where I urged her to stay and be safe while I handled things.

"Okay," I said. "But I don't know what we're going to do."

Holding hands, we stepped out into the passageway. About ten feet away were Fletcher and Grif.

"Well," Fletcher drawled, "look who's here."

"What do you guys want?" I asked.

"One last look at the competition, maybe."

"I don't think so."

If we'd been in a saloon, right about now people would be giving us room. All we needed was music building in the background.

Fletcher shook his finger at me. "You have pissed me off all summer, do you know that?"

"C'mon. Take your buddy and get out of here. Go sober up."

"Don't tell me what to do, you little sonofabitch!"

He stumbled toward us. Cara squeezed my hand so hard I thought my nails were going to bleed.

"Look at you," he said scornfully. "Standin' behind some little girl."

I glanced down at our boots, Cara Mae's and mine. "Actually," I said, fighting to keep my voice steady, "we're standing side by side."

"C'mon," Grif said, "forget it."

The creature could talk! And it was the flutiest little voice. No wonder he never said anything.

"You forget it," Fletcher roared.

"Look, you guys," I said quietly. "Either get out of here or Cara runs down to the guard shack. It's that simple."

"And what if we run after her?" Fletcher mimicked prissily.

"You're too drunk and Grif is too slow."

"So while she's gone we just kick your ass good."

"You do," said Cara Mae firmly, "and you go to jail for assault."

"And while the cops are booking you they find the

204

hypo or the pills or whatever it was you were going to slip our filly."

I could see Grif look at his partner.

"You didn't even plan this, did you?" I said. "You just got high and started to think about tomorrow and thought you'd try. Well, it's not going to work. So why don't you get out of here and let our horse get some rest."

"C'mon," piped Grif. "We'll beat 'em, anyway."

Fletcher was swaying like an elm in a high wind. "I hate that little sonofabitch," he said, meaning me. "I just want to put him in the hospital."

"There's always later," Grif squeaked, looking right at me.

"I'll be here," I said, sounding braver than I felt. "All night."

Grif tugged at his buddy's arm. "C'mon," he said, still sounding like Mickey Mouse.

"Tha' little shrimp," said Fletcher, turning away.

"I may be little," I said, almost to myself, "but I took care of you."

Cara Mae and I watched until they rounded the corner at the end of shed row. Then we heard a truck start and glide away.

"Holy shit," I said, leaning into her.

She put her arms around me. "Come on inside."

"Now I know," I said sitting down, "what people mean when they say 'I need a drink.' "

"You were great." She hugged me.

"You, too. It was smart to say you'd have him arrested. I thought for a minute there I was a goner."

"You think they'll come back?"

"Who knows."

"Maybe we better stay up and watch, though."

"For a little while, anyway."

She walked over and sat on the other cot. "A refrigerator?" she asked, pointing to the corner.

"Lew's idea of roughing it."

"Where is Lew, anyway?"

"Oh, his dad kidnapped him for his birthday. They're out in the desert about a hundred miles from here."

"So we're all alone with nothing to do." She picked up one of Lew's magazines. "We could always read. See, the July *Soldier of Fortune*. I must have missed that one."

I sat down beside her. "I don't want to read. I've read enough."

When I woke up, the blanket had slipped off both of us. Cara was curled up on the cot right beside mine with her back to me and both hands clamped between her knees. It was still dark out, but the backstretch — just like always — was beginning to stir.

"Should we get up?" I whispered, touching her shoulder.

"Uh-huh." She rolled over.

When I kissed her lightly she turned away a little. "Does my mouth taste bad?"

"No, it's fine."

She swung her legs out and slipped into her panties, then stood up, turned around shyly, and reached for her bra.

"You're just as pretty from the back," I observed.

"I was talking to my dad," she said, blushing, "when we were packing up yesterday. About when he was sixteen and in Montana. Kids didn't used to do this, I guess."

"Spend the night together?" I stood up, too, and looked for my jeans.

"Yeah. I'm glad we did though. It's nice." She turned toward me. "I mean it was nice with you."

I looked around. "Not exactly every girl's dream."

"I don't know. I'm never gonna walk in another stall and feel the same." She smiled and picked up her hat. "Let's go look at that filly."

"You want to go out alone?"

"I'm not ashamed of anything, are you?"

"No," I said firmly. "Let's go."

"In a way," she said without moving, "I wish we didn't have to, though. I kind of wish we could just stay here all day."

"Why not? There's almost nobody around."

She shook her head. "Mr. Solomon wants me to gallop this colt of his so he can run him Wednesday at Turf Paradise."

"What about afterward? I could wait here and fix us something . . ."

"Got to help my dad some more."

I opened the half-door for her. "I guess I'll see you tonight, then. At the saddling paddock?"

"Sure. For sure."

It wasn't like a chill had set in, but the real world had definitely stepped between us.

"Do you want, uh, coffee or anything?"

"No, I'd better . . . you know, go on over there."

"Sure, okay." I shrugged helplessly. "See you."

" 'Bye." She held one hand out and — what else could I do — I shook it.

When I got home, Wes was standing at the counter in his underwear.

"How do you get your T-shirts to do that?" I asked.

"Do what?"

"Not be wrinkled."

"I have them pressed."

"And your shorts?"

"And my shorts."

"And your socks?"

"Of course not. What do you think I am, a fanatic?"

"What are you doing up this early, anyway?"

"Oh, I just got home and I couldn't sleep."

Just got home. "Alex?"

Wes sighed happily. "That's his name." Then he poured more coffee and offered me some, but I shook my head.

"I think I should sleep some more."

"Everything go all right last night?"

"Nothing I couldn't handle."

He looked at me critically. "There's more here than meets these old eyes, isn't there?"

"Maybe," I said innocently.

"Anyway, the big race is tonight, correct? If you're out late, what's the plan in the morning?"

I shrugged. "Train's at eight."

"Is Cara coming?"

"No. Her dad wants to leave early, too."

"Lew?"

"I don't think goodbyes are Lew's style."

"Then it's just you and me, babe."

"That's okay." I stood up and took a step or two toward my bedroom.

"I can't believe," Wes said, "that you'll be gone tomorrow and things will go back to what I loosely refer to as normal."

"I thought I'd really want to go home. And I do," I added in a hurry, "but I don't."

"And I thought I'd want you to." Then he shrugged, turned around, and began to wash the cup he was holding in his hand.

14

I got to the track early that afternoon, said hi to a couple of outriders, waved to Jack, who was talking on the phone, and went by The Dark Mirage. She seemed a little on edge but basically fine.

I was cleaning out the tack room when Lew showed up.

"What the hell happened to you last night?"

He balanced unsteadily on one foot. "A fucking rattlesnake bit me in the boot, man." He pointed and grinned.

"I know where you were. I mean why didn't you tell your old man to go jump? Why weren't you here with me?"

"Hey," he said, sounding hurt, "you know I'm always on Red Alert. And anyway, Edgar kidnapped me for my birthday."

"Oh, bullshit. If I can tell my dad I want to go to college and major in horses, you can at least tell yours you've got something better to do than play soldier all the time."

"You really going to major in horses?"

"I think so. Remember those brochures I had from the U.?"

"When did you tell your folks?"

"Well, I haven't exactly told them yet." I stepped out into the sun. "But I'm going to."

Lew laughed and punched me lightly in the shoulder. "I really got to put a lid on Edgar," he said thoughtfully.

"Why didn't you think of that last night?"

"Why? What happened?"

"Fletcher and Grif came by."

"No shit! Was it like the gunfight at the OK Corral?"

"Not exactly. We just yelled at each other. But the filly's fine."

He looked at the ground then. "I'm sorry I let you down."

"Forget it. Things worked out all right."

"You're not pissed?"

I thought of standing up to Fletcher and Grif. I thought of making love to Cara Mae.

"No."

"Where's Cara?" Lew asked as we fussed over the horse. "It's an hour till post time."

"She'll be here."

"What's her story, anyway?"

"We had this argument. Everything's fine now."

He arched his bleached eyebrows suggestively. "Did you make up?"

"Yeah, Lew. We made up."

Just then Jack appeared. "Ready, boys?"

Lew eyed him curiously, then leaned over and tried to peer under Jack's gray Stetson.

"Why aren't you wearing your lucky rug?"

211

"Ah, I lost the goddamn thing playing poker."

Lew looked amazed. "You bet your best toupee?"

Jack frowned and jammed both hands into his pockets. "We going to run this horse or not?"

I remembered my first time in the receiving barn, holding up Moon's Medicine, who was now dead and gone. I remembered standing there in my high-tops, seeing Cara Mae and already liking her.

As we led The Dark Mirage down the long gauntlet of curious horseplayers, I remembered how it'd been that first night at the track, how I'd studied every move that Lew made as he helped saddle, and later how I'd peered enviously into the walking ring as Jack talked to the jockey, then put him up, patted him on the boot, and wished him good luck.

"They're staring at us," Lew said, nodding toward Fletcher and Grif.

I pulled the cinch on the saddle tight. "Let's don't get paranoid."

"You boys come on along this time," said Jack.

We looked at each other. "In the walking ring?" I asked.

"You're the ones got her this far."

"Cara should be here, then."

"Fine with me. Where is she?"

"Look!" said Lew, pointing like a hunter.

Sure enough, and running, the way I'd seen her do a hundred times, head down, holding her hat on.

"Hi," she said breathlessly. "I had to find my best shirt, and then traffic was screwed up."

"Let's get a move on," said Jack before I could kiss her.

I'd always stood in the crowd, looking in at the horses and trainers and owners and jockeys. But inside the walking ring, it was like the eye of some gentle storm, the only quiet place as people and animals circled and milled outside us.

"Her owner's not here tonight?" I asked as Lew led The Dark Mirage past us.

"She's just a figure on a tax sheet somewhere, Billy," Jack replied.

So someone owned her but didn't care about her, didn't care if she won or lost, really, as long as he could write her off at the end of the year.

Jack motioned for Pedroza, the rider, to come a little closer. Then he introduced Lew and Cara and me. "Go ahead and handle this, Billy. You know the horse better'n I do."

The jockey looked up at me expectantly. I looked at Cara Mae.

"You tell him, okay? You're the rider."

Cara licked her lips and adjusted her hat. "Well," she said firmly, "the last time I worked her, she was great; I think the only difference was she'd finally calmed down. So try and keep her away from the other horses and have the starter put her in the gate last. If she gets nervous, we're sunk."

Pedroza nodded and adjusted his helmet as Jack pointed at The Dark Mirage. "Billy, this is your show. Go ahead and put him on."

I touched Cara on the elbow and the three of us walked across the springy grass. The jockey slipped between the horse and me, cocked one leg, and glanced back.

I looked at Cara Mae.

"Jack's right, Billy. You do it."

"Good luck," I said as he settled himself. He grinned, kissed his thumb, and made the sign of the cross as the outrider led them away.

"You looked good doing that," Cara said, linking her arm through mine.

I remembered more than two months before, standing with Lew at the walking ring and watching Jack put Pedroza on Moon's Medicine. I heard myself say, "I'd like to do that," and Lew replied that there was no way. But it had happened.

"Let's go," I said to Cara, squeezing her hand. "This is one race we don't want to miss."

Inside, Cara Mae led me to the nearest line.

"This one's shorter."

"No. C'mon!"

"Is this lucky or something?" I asked, stepping in behind her.

"Or something."

I looked up at the big neon board. Fletcher and Grif's horse was seven-to-one. Ours was nineteen-to-one. If she won, she'd pay right around forty dollars.

"Are you betting?" I asked as we shuffled forward.

"Nope. At least not any more than I already have."

"Why are we in line?"

"You'll see."

Just then it was her turn. Cara stepped up to the window and leaned in.

"Daddy," she said, "I want you to meet Billy Kennedy. He's the boy I told you about." Then she tugged at my sleeve.

"This is your dad?" I whispered, taking off my hat.

"Get on up there. He won't bite."

"Hi," I said, half peeking around her. "Nice to meet you."

Clerks work behind windows with little bars so people can't just reach in and grab the money. I stuck my fingers through, anyway, to show that I was willing to shake hands. He looked down at them curiously.

"Hello," he said.

"Hey," someone shouted. "Move it up there."

"Want to bet?" he asked.

"Why not? Six dollars to win on the seven."

Cara Mae leaned in as I reached for the ticket. "'Bye, Daddy."

"Goodbye, sir."

"Don't be late tonight, hear? I want to get an early start tomorrow."

"Yes, sir," we said in unison.

"Why didn't you tell me?" I asked once we were clear of the line. "I would've cut my hair or something."

"Mostly," she said, pausing by the door that separated the air-conditioned grandstand from the rest of the world, "I didn't want you to go home and never meet my dad."

I shoved the metal handle and we stepped out into the heat and the noise. "I'm glad you wanted me to," I said. "I didn't think about it much, but every now and then I'd wonder if there was something wrong with me. Or him."

"I'm slow to trust people," she said, "but I get there eventually."

"You and The Dark Mirage."

She looked toward the track as she weighed the comparison. Then she took my hand. Across the way we could see Pedroza's scarlet silks, the filly's gleaming coat, and the proud way she carried herself.

"I guess I am at that."

As the horses loaded into the gate I thought of my dad and how, at the first of every month, he said he just pulled the plug and the dollars drained away. I wondered if my two hundred dollars would do that, trickle into Fletcher's deep pocket. I resolved to not even tell my folks. I would just say that I hadn't been able to save as much as I'd hoped.

"Oh God," said Abby, raising both sets of crossed fingers.

"Keep her head straight," Cara muttered.

"Pop the gate, sweetheart," said Lew. "I need that hundred bucks."

"They're off!" boomed the announcer.

"Damn! She came out slow."

"We knew she'd do that, Lew."

"But French Bred is layin' third."

There was no denying that. Fletcher's filly was just off the front-runners while we were ten lengths back.

"She'll never make it," he groaned.

"Hold on. It isn't over yet."

As they made the long turn for home, the early speed started to come back. Pedroza had made up a couple of lengths and I could see the rider on French Bred uncock his stick and go to work.

"She could do it," Cara said tensely. "She could do it."

Fletcher's filly was running just like she worked out — at the same speed the whole way. But our horse was picking them off one by one. Another three lengths and she'd pass her.

"C'mon, Dark Mirage," Cara pleaded. "C'mon."

Two hundred yards from the wire, just about where we were standing, we took her, surging past French Bred.

"All right!"

Lew and I exchanged high fives, low fives, and all the fives in between. Abby kissed me, knocking my hat off. Then Cara and I found each other.

"We won!" she said, kissing me. "We won!"

We kissed and kept kissing, but even in the middle of it I was wondering if this would be the last time, if we weren't already saying goodbye.

Just then Jack pushed his way through a crowd at the bar. He had a towering redhead with him and he was waving a handful of money.

"That guard who was holding this took off for Phoenix already, so he gave it to me for safekeeping. But it's all yours now." He held it out enticingly. "Who gets it?"

"Give it to Cara," I said, a little out of breath.

"No, you take it."

I'd never held a thousand dollars before, so I let it lie

there in my hand a few seconds before I divided it up. Lew and Abby were hopping around as Cara Mae grinned.

"We'd better get The Dark Mirage and cool her out," I said.

"Do that," Jack urged, "and lock things up for me, okay?" He turned away, then back again. "If we miss each other, Billy, I'll see you sooner or later." He held out his hand. "Horseplayers always run into each other."

"I sure hope so. Thanks for everything."

"You know, kid," he said, still pumping, "you did a hell of a job."

"Seems like I did a lot of sitting around with a stop-watch while Cara rode."

He smiled. "You're the one thought to get that filly away from the backstretch for a little while. And even if you hadn't, you got common sense and you ain't afraid of hard work. Few more years of gettin' stepped on, crapped on, and bit, you could work for anybody anywhere."

"Who could resist an offer like that," I said, and everybody laughed.

The Dark Mirage was on her toes, so Cara Mae took a tight hold.

"Do you think she knows she did okay?" Lew said.

I patted her hard on the neck; she turned and took a half-hearted nip at me.

"I think she knows she's hungry."

Halfway back to the barn, we ran into a lynch mob. About twenty cowboys had Fletcher and Grif up against a shed.

"I'll pay you boys," Fletcher oozed. "It's just gonna take a little time, that's all."

"That ain't the way it works, Fletch old boy. And you know it."

"Hey, now. Settle down. Have I ever welshed on a bet before?"

"Hell, yes," said three or four men in unison.

"And," somebody hollered, "I'm not leaving here without my money."

"String 'em up!" shouted Lew.

"There's the ones," Fletcher yelled. "They probably drugged my filly so she couldn't run. I say we wait and settle all this when the lab tests come back."

"And that won't work either," someone said, sounding disgusted. "You lost, now pay up."

"Let's go," I said, "before this filly cords up on us."

"Look," said Lew as I got out the bucket and the brushes for the last time. "Abby and I kind of want to bet the Derby. You can do this by yourself."

Cara Mae glanced at me and grinned.

"No long, tearful goodbyes, okay, Lew?" I said. "I can't take too much emotion."

"Oh, hell," said Abby. "Jack's right. We'll bump into each other again."

"Sure."

Abby put her arms around me, then Cara Mae.

"No hugging, Billy," Lew warned.

"Who wants to hug you," I said, pointing the hose at him.

We shook hands then, letting it develop into a squeezing contest.

"Okay, okay," Lew squealed. "Take it easy or I'll never shoot another mutant."

"Go watch the Derby, Lew."

"You like anybody?" he asked over his shoulder.

I shook my head, and when he turned and looked at Cara Mae expectantly, she just shrugged.

The two of us cooled The Dark Mirage out, walking in the familiar circle, one on each side of her, our hands just touching as we held on to the halter. While Cara Mae let her drink, I mixed some Guinness in her mash as a special treat.

Finally I checked the doors to the office and tack room, and looked in the stalls to make sure nothing Jack needed had been left behind.

"See you," I murmured to the horse, but she was grinding away with those big yellow teeth."

Cara and I had covered about twenty yards when I stopped and turned around. I'd painted every inch of that wood, swept the hard-packed dirt a hundred times, walked a dozen horses in a thousand circles.

Cara put her hand on my arm. "You gonna miss this ugly place?" she asked.

"Yes," I said. "I am."

We were riding in the white van for the last time. Tomorrow it would have Indian Arts painted across both sides, and Wes would take it to Taos to buy some more of those beautifully flawed rugs he'd told Lew and me about.

"Do you want the air conditioning on?" I asked as we crept along in the homebound traffic.

"No, thanks."

"Radio?"

"Billy, I'm fine." She reached across and her left hand settled on my shoulder.

The moon was out, so huge and clear I could see the outlines of the craters and dry lakes. If my folks were up, they were looking at the same reflected light. Were they talking about me? I wondered. On the phone, Dad had said they were looking forward to having me home again. But their summer was over too. I'll bet a part of them liked being alone together and would miss it.

Cara Mae was on her third or fourth cigarette — lighting one, putting it out, lighting another — when I asked her what she was going to do with the money she'd won.

"Maybe save up for a horse of my own. What about you?" I followed her eyes to the big green sign beside the interstate: Shadow Road.

"Put it in the bank, I guess." I eased over to the right and took the off-ramp. Behind me, somebody honked and flashed his lights.

Cara Mae turned, shielding her eyes. "What's his problem?"

"I'm driving about six miles an hour."

A hundred yards away was the mailbox with Whitney painted on it and, just beyond that, the faint ruts we'd cut going up the hill every night.

"Do you know what I'd really like to do right now?"

I said. "Drive you all the way home, right up to the front door."

She grinned and made a sweeping help-yourself gesture. We'd no more than eased around the huge wall of oleanders when the curtains on the front window slid back and there was her father's thin, pale face. Cara waved and I sort of lifted one hand off the steering wheel. The curtain closed slowly, like the big ones do when the play is over.

I turned off the engine and looked around.

"Not much, is it," she said.

"Is this the place you never wanted me to see? It's not so bad."

"Looks better at night."

I adjusted the mirror, adjusted my hat, adjusted the mirror again. I looked down at my hands. Three months ago they were pale and smooth, but not anymore.

Then we just sat there in the moonlight. All of a sudden I felt terrible. I'd pictured this scene a hundred times and seventy-five of those we were in the back of the van doing things I'd only heard about. The other twenty-five we were either very brave and one of us called the other one darling, or we clung to one another, promising to write and count the days till next summer.

Now, when it was happening, all I felt was like crying. I swallowed hard. *No crying*, I said to myself. *You're not dressed for crying. You're wearing that hat and those boots. So don't even think about it.*

"I was talking to my dad," she said, "about you and me and how I felt and all and he said, "Honey, you're

222

gonna be in love a thousand times before you're done.'
Do you think that's true?"

"No."

She shook her head slowly. "I don't either. Not the
way I feel tonight, anyway."

"We could write," I said feebly.

She stroked my shirt like it was part of me. "I hate to
write, Billy. Essays and all that stuff — it's just like pul-
lin' teeth."

"I've got all this money now. If I gave you some, would
you call me? I'd call you, but you haven't got a number
yet."

"I never thought about that."

"What if I give you my number. Just in case." I patted
all my pockets. I had a pen, but no paper. I leaned past
her and popped open the glove compartment. Nearly
empty.

"Here," she said, rolling up the sleeve on her best
shirt, the one with the fringe shimmying above her small,
perfect breasts.

"Where?"

"On my arm. I'll write it down when I get inside."

I pressed into the soft skin, careful not to hurt her.
Then she turned her arm and read.

"Nice number," she whispered. "Lots of sevens."

Just then the porch light flashed off and on, the ancient
signal of fathers everywhere trying to get their daughters
inside so they could go to sleep.

"I'm home all the time," I said. "I never go anywhere.
So just pick up the phone whenever."

"Okay." She smiled, leaning over to kiss me.

For the last time I took off my hat so I wouldn't put her eye out. That was something else I wouldn't have to do anymore, wouldn't *get* to do anymore."

"I think I'm gonna die," I said into her shoulder.

"No, you're not," she replied softly.

"If I do, will you take my body to Phoenix with you?"

"You're great," she said, pulling away and grinning bravely. "It was a great summer."

She touched the brim of her hat politely, then slid out of the van, ran up the three concrete blocks that doubled as steps, and closed the door behind her.

15

"Got everything?" Wes asked as I opened the car door.

I showed him my suitcase.

"Pitiful. You look like you're going to live at the orphanage."

"I threw away all those striped shirts, remember?"

"You had a red-and-white one that made you look like a barber pole when you blushed."

"Except that all the stripes on my shirts went up and down because I was trying to look tall."

"What made you decide you were tall enough after all?"

I shrugged. "I'm as tall as I am. It's okay."

"I liked it when you blushed all the time. It was cute."

"I think the suntan hides it now. I still get embarrassed."

"By the way, do you have any condoms?"

I stared at him. "For the train?"

"I just wanted to see one more blush for old times' sake."

Laughing and shaking my head, I closed the door, adjusted the seat belt, and fiddled with my sunglasses —

the ones he'd bought me in June — as we made our way out of Nuevo Grande.

"Why do you look different to me today?" I asked.

"You mean the bolo tie?"

"And all the bracelets."

"Tourists seem to like to buy things right off the trader, so I have to wear half a display case at a time. And just after Labor Day this place starts crawling with snowbirds."

"What are snowbirds, anyway? Cara talked about them and I didn't want to look dumb, so I didn't ask." And where was Cara now? Probably just outside of town, riding with her boot braced against the battered dashboard and staring out the window.

"Snowbirds are people who live in the East and can afford to come out here for the winter."

We turned right where River Road meets Oracle. Left led toward Phoenix. If we went that way and drove fast, we could overtake Cara Mae and her dad.

"I told her," I said abruptly.

"Told her what?"

"That I loved her."

"Ah, good."

"You were right about that. Telling her, I mean. You were right about a lot of things." I turned toward him, pulling the seat belt away from me. "Can I ask you one more question?"

"Of course."

"Cara was talking to her dad about how she felt about me, and he said she'd be in love a thousand times. Do you think that's true? I mean for me, too? For every-body?"

"I know what he means," Wes said thoughtfully. "And he's probably right. But," he added, taking his eyes off the road for an instant and looking right at me, "that doesn't help much today, does it?"

We stood together on the platform and waited for the train, but this time I waited in the shade. No more fainting for this kid.

"I gave you back the house keys and the car keys, right?"

"Check."

"Listen! There's the whistle."

How many Westerns had I seen where guys were waiting for the train. Who would get off this one — mail-order brides or grizzled killers?

"Cute," said Wes as guys in LaCoste T-shirts and girls in shorts and sandals poured through the narrow doors, waving for their luggage and blinking in the sun.

I looked down at myself — scuffed boots and faded jeans, Wrangler shirt already fraying at the cuffs. Then I took off my hat, the one Moon's Medicine had almost stepped on, the one I'd sweated in and tossed in the back seat before I kissed Cara Mae. "Keep this for me, will you? I'll wear the boots in Bradleyville, but probably not the hat."

"Sure. I'll put it in your closet. It'll be there when you come back."

"I might, too," I said, picking up my suitcase. "Even before college."

"Anytime, kiddo."

"Just be here, okay? I mean . . . just be here."

"I'll do my best."

I dropped the suitcase and put my arms around him.

"I'll pat you so heartily," he whispered, "that we'll look like two he-men and not one straight teenager and one forty-year-old sissy."

"I don't care about that. Honest."

He held me at arm's length. Behind us the train creaked.

"Don't miss the sonofabitch," he said, grinning. "I can't do this again for the 6:05."

I handed my bag to a porter, who made room for me on the bottom step. Wes walked alongside the train as it picked up speed.

"Say hi to everybody," he reminded me.

"Okay. See you. Thanks for everything."

He stopped then and lifted one hand. Before I could wave back, the train lurched and I had to hold on. Then by the time I made my way through the first cars and found a seat by a window, it was too late to wave. We were almost out of town and I was really on my way.